Mel Bay Presents

# BACH

## Three Sonatas & Three Partitas for Solo Violin, BWV 1001-1006

---

### Includes the Performance Practice essay:

## Performing Bach

---

### Scholarly Performing Edition by

## Lawrence Golan

1 2 3 4 5 6 7 8 9 0

© 2006 BY MEL BAY PUBLICATIONS, INC., PACIFIC, MO 63069.
ALL RIGHTS RESERVED. INTERNATIONAL COPYRIGHT SECURED. B.M.I. MADE AND PRINTED IN U.S.A.
No part of this publication may be reproduced in whole or in part, in a retrieval system, or transmitted in any form
or by any means, electronic, mechanical, photocopy, recording, or otherwise, without written permission of the publisher.

**Visit us on the Web at www.melbay.com — E-mail us at email@melbay.com**

# Table of Contents

Preface .................................................................................................................................................. iii

Sonata No. 1 in g minor, BWV 1001 .................................................................................................. 1

Partita No. 1 in b minor, BWV 1002 ................................................................................................... 8

Sonata No. 2 in a minor, BWV 1003 ................................................................................................. 18

Partita No. 2 in d minor, BWV 1004 ................................................................................................. 28

Sonata No. 3 in C Major, BWV 1005 ............................................................................................... 40

Partita No. 3 in E Major, BWV 1006 ................................................................................................ 52

Performing Bach: Introduction ......................................................................................................... 61

Dotted Rhythms ................................................................................................................................ 63

    Sonata No. 1 in g minor ............................................................................................................ 67

    Partita No. 1 in b minor ............................................................................................................ 68

    Sonata No. 2 in a minor ............................................................................................................ 70

    Partita No. 2 in d minor ............................................................................................................ 70

    Sonata No. 3 in C Major ........................................................................................................... 72

    Partita No. 3 in E Major ........................................................................................................... 73

Trills .................................................................................................................................................. 75

    Sonata No. 1 in g minor ............................................................................................................ 77

    Partita No. 1 in b minor ............................................................................................................ 78

    Sonata No. 2 in a minor ............................................................................................................ 78

    Partita No. 2 in d minor ............................................................................................................ 78

    Sonata No. 3 in C Major ........................................................................................................... 79

    Partita No. 3 in E Major ........................................................................................................... 79

Appendix A: Vibrato ......................................................................................................................... 80

Appendix B: Fingerings .................................................................................................................... 81

Appendix C: Bowing Styles .............................................................................................................. 81

Appendix D: Ritardandos .................................................................................................................. 82

Appendix E: Quantz/C.P.E. Bach; German Text ............................................................................... 83

Bibliography ...................................................................................................................................... 85

# Preface
## Johann Sebastian Bach

Three Sonatas and Three Partitas for Solo Violin, BWV 1001-1006
Scholarly-Performing Edition by Lawrence Golan

A facsimile of Bach's autograph manuscript was used in the preparation of this edition and the composer's intentions have been preserved to the last detail. Of particular note is the fact that all stems have been beamed together as they appear in the autograph manuscript. This is of great importance when making interpretive decisions regarding dotted rhythms. Helpful fingering and bowing suggestions are provided by the editor, but are clearly distinguished from Bach's original notation, allowing the performer the freedom to accept or reject any given suggestion. Furthermore, the volume comes complete with Dr. Golan's essay "Performing Bach: Dotted Rhythms and Trills in the Sonatas and Partitas for Solo Violin," which also includes scholarly discussions of vibrato, fingerings, bowing styles, and ritardandos in Baroque music. The inclusion of this comprehensive study of Baroque performance practices makes this edition a must for any violinist interested in performing the Bach Sonatas and Partitas in an historically informed manner.

**Fingering Suggestions:**

- All fingerings are editorial suggestions and do not appear in the autograph manuscript (except for those in Partita No. 3, Gavotte en Rondeaux, m. 34, which do appear in the autograph manuscript).

- Each movement begins in 1st position unless otherwise indicated.

- Fingerings have only been marked to indicate a change of position or an enharmonic fingering that does not necessitate an actual shift.

- It is implied that the performer remain in any given position, including half position, until the next marked fingering.

- A circled fingering indicates a stretch rather than a shift of positions.

- An open string indicates a shift to 1st position unless otherwise indicated.

- Regarding open strings vs. 4th fingers in 1st position, only 4th fingers have been marked. If there is no 4, then an open string is intended -- unless the note is part of a chord for which 4th finger is the only possibility.

**Bowing Suggestions:**

- All solid slurs are original and do appear in the autograph manuscript.

- All segmented slurs, articulation dots or dashes, as well as down-bow and up-bow symbols are editorial suggestions and do not appear in the autograph manuscript.

- Each movement begins down-bow unless otherwise indicated.

- A segmented slur combined with a dash indicates a slight separation between the notes.

- A segmented slur combined with a dot indicates more separation between the notes than one with a dash.

**Dynamics:**

- All dynamics are original and do appear in the autograph manuscript (except for the forte in Partita No. 2, Giga, m. 27, which has been added in parentheses to match m. 12).

- When writing piano, Bach sometimes wrote P and other times partially wrote the word out (e.g. pia.). These differences have been maintained, but in cases of the latter, the publishers have completed the word in italics.

- In Partita No. 3, Preludio, mm. 63 and 65, the editor suggests moving the dynamic marking to the third 16th-note of the measure to match the dynamic scheme in mm. 13 and 15.

**Trills:**

- All trills, exept those in parentheses, are original and do appear in the autograph manuscript.

- All trills in parentheses are editorial suggestions.

**Footnotes:**

- All astericks and corresponding footnotes are editorial and do not appear in the autograph manuscript.

**"Arpeggio" in the Ciaccona:**

- In Partita No. 2, Ciaccona, m. 89, beat 2, Bach clearly wrote the word "arpeggio" to instruct the performer to continue the arpeggio pattern that he established at the beginning of the measure. While this pattern works for 3-note chords, it must be altered to execute 4-note chords. The editor suggests the following execution: for each chord, roll from bottom to top and back twice, repeating both the top and bottom notes each time. In addition, it is suggested that this execution commences on beat 2 of m. 101 (even though the chords still contain only 3 notes) so that the new arpeggio pattern coincides with the beginning of the phrase.

**Fermatas:**

- The fermata symbols on the final double bar or repeat sign of many of the movements are as they appear in the facsimile of Bach's autograph manuscript. Essentially, the fermatas indicate the end of a movement.

# Sonata No. 1
BWV 1001

✼ This figure appears as a dotted 16th - note and three 64th - notes (a mathematical impossibility) in the autograph manuscript. See Lawrence Golan, "Performing Bach," p. 67 for an explanation.

Siciliana

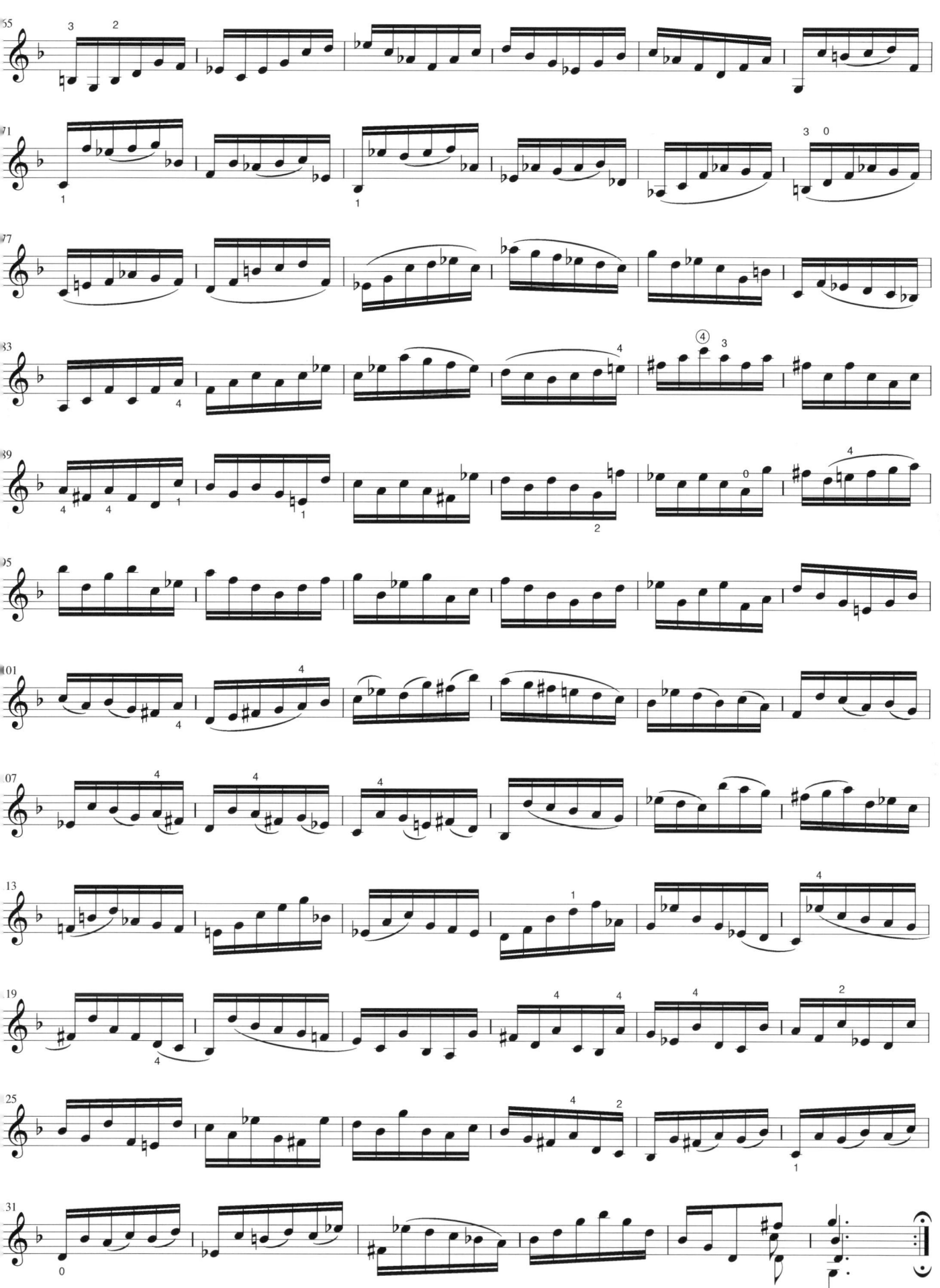

# Partita No. 1
BWV 1002

Allemanda

# Sonata No. 2
BWV 1003

※ These wavy lines are not trill symbols. They are most likely signs indicating vibrato, which can be executed with either the left hand *or the bow*. See Lawrence Golan, "Performing Bach," p. 78.

# Partita No. 2
## BWV 1004

Allemanda

※ The dotted rhythms in this movement may be performed with a 2:1 ratio. See Lawrence Golan, "Performing Bach," p. 71.
※※ This chord appears as a dotted quarter-note in the autograph manuscript.

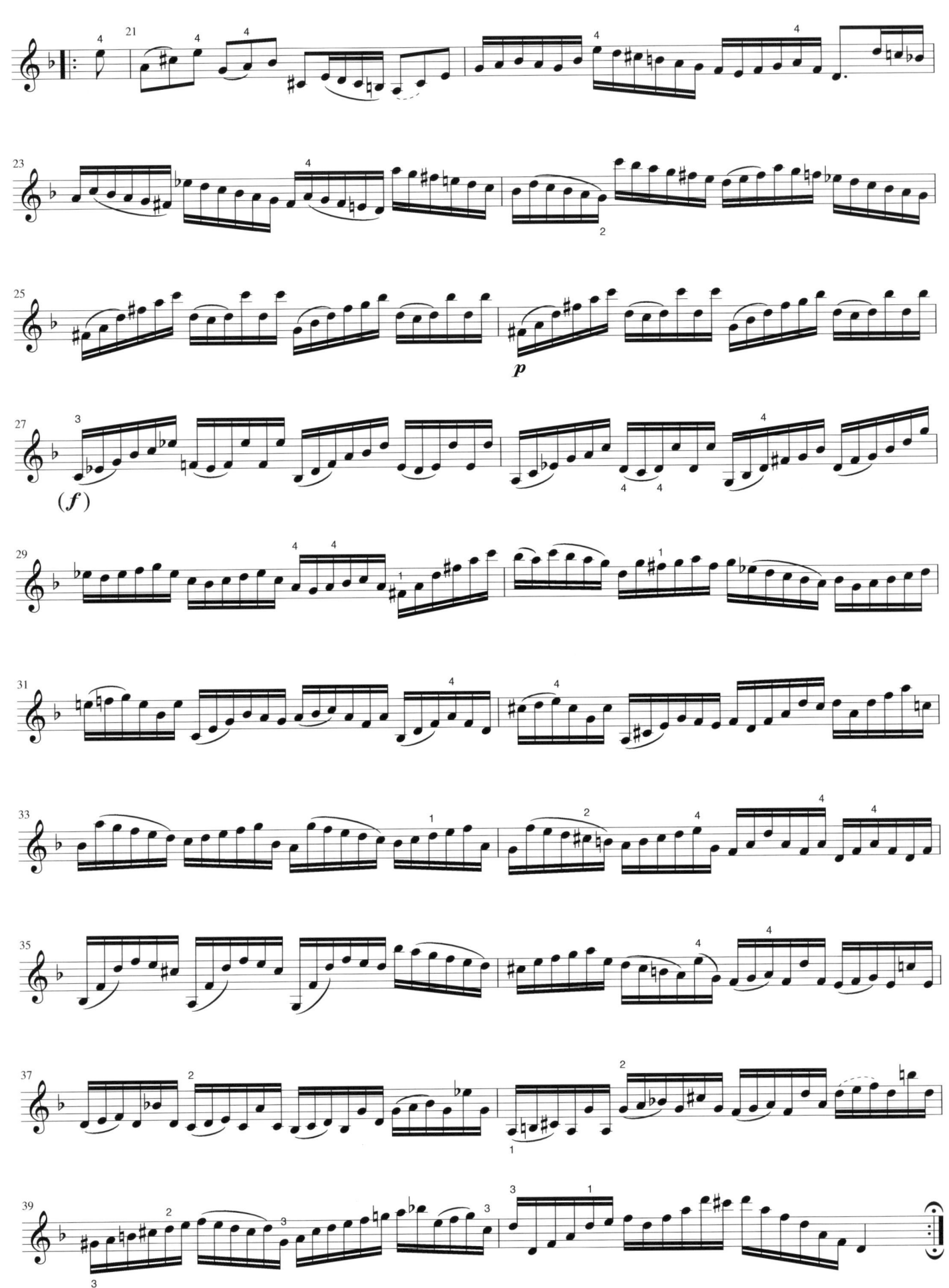

Ciaccona

*　See preface, "Arpeggio" in the Ciaccona, for suggested execution.
**　The performer may wish to play open D with this chord, instead of the A that is printed.
***　With this fingering, the open A is intended to be played only on the first down-bow; a 3-note chord, D -D -F♯, being played thereafter.

※ In this measure, the performer may wish to omit the G-string D and play only the open D.

# Sonata No. 3
## BWV 1005

✵ The editor suggests that for consistency, all ♩. ♪ figures in this movement be slurred. They have been printed here, however, as they appear in the autograph manuscript.

Fuga

※ In the autograph manuscript there is no ♮ in front of the F. However, the fact that this measure is analogous to m. 279 and that there are other instances of missing accidentals in the autograph manuscript lead the editor to believe that this should probably be F♮.

※ See Lawrence Golan, "Performing Bach," p. 79 for the suggested execution of this trill.

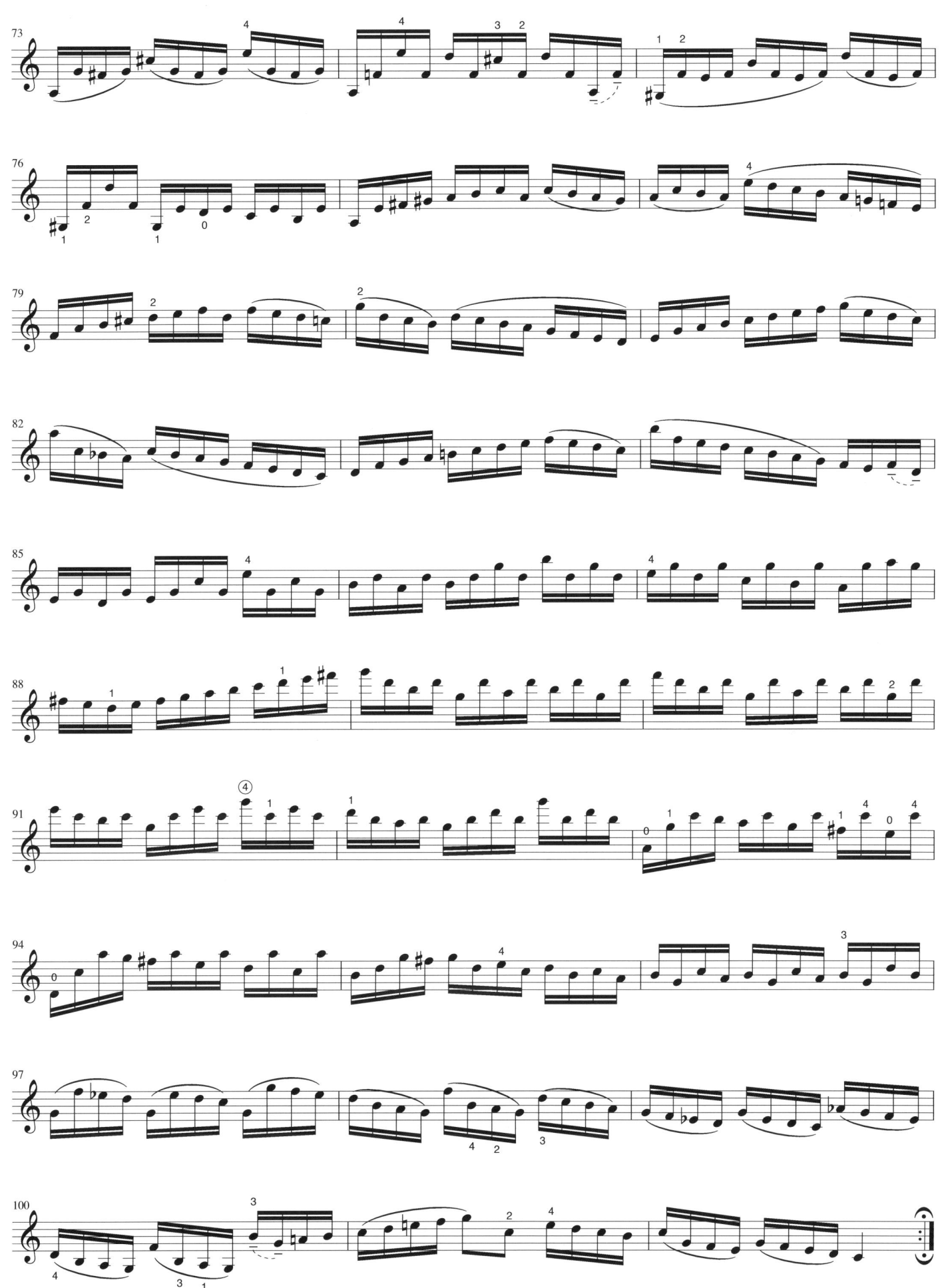

# Partita No. 3
BWV 1006

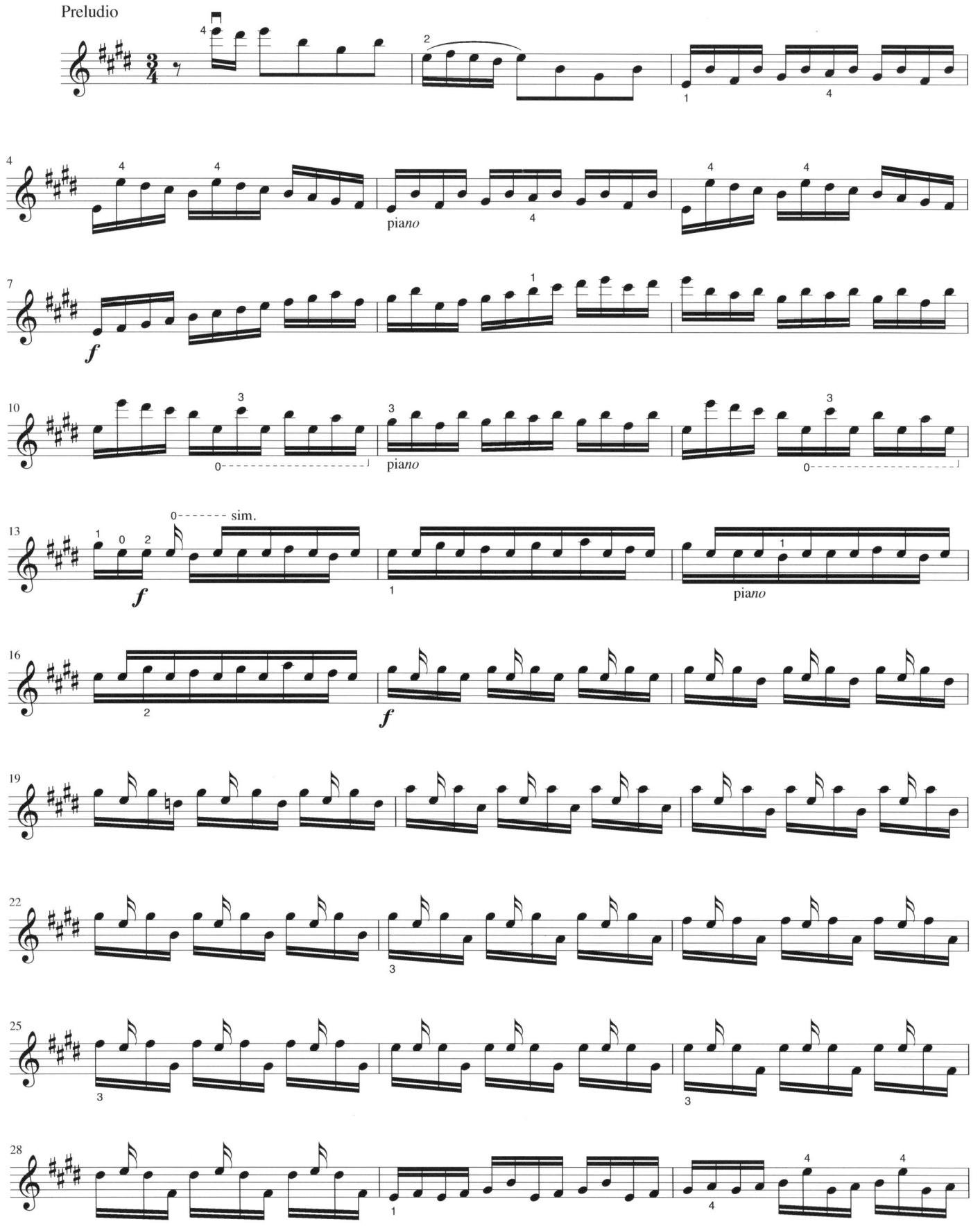

※ The editor suggests that for consistency, the performer remove the first two slurs in this measure.
※※ See preface regarding dynamics.

✻ See preface regarding dynamics.

* This dotted rest appears as a simple half-note rest in the autograph manuscript.
** Plural spelling of Rondeau as per the autograph manuscript.

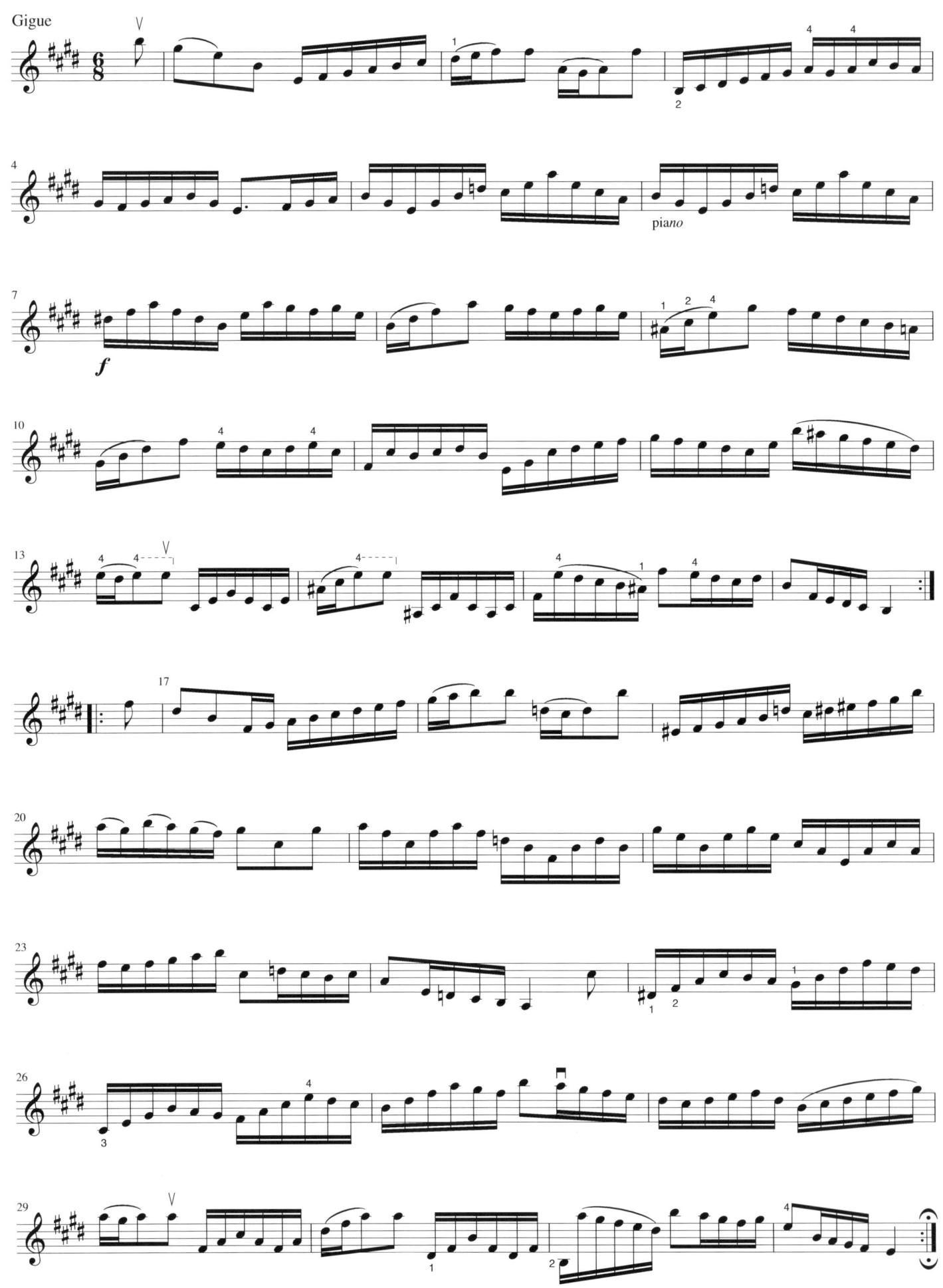

# *Performing Bach:*

*Dotted Rhythms and Trills
in the
Sonatas and Partitas
for Solo Violin*

*by
Lawrence Golan*

*Also includes scholarly discussions of vibrato, fingerings, bowing styles, and ritardandos in Baroque music*

# Performing Bach:
# Dotted Rhythms and Trills
# in the Sonatas and Partitas for Solo Violin

## by
## Lawrence Golan

When performing a piece of music, one of our primary concerns should be to present the work the way the composer intended it. This can be done by using urtext editions, following the composer's instructions diligently, and being aware of performance practice issues associated with the composer or style of music in question. However, as 21st century musicians, much of the music we perform was written over three hundred years ago, and as time passes it becomes increasingly difficult to know exactly how a composer intended his or her music to be performed. Such is the case with Johann Sebastian Bach and other composers of the Baroque era.

Over the past several decades, musicologists have devoted increasing amounts of attention to what is variably known as "Baroque Performance Practice" or "Historical Authenticity." Through the study of contemporary treatises, instruments, paintings, autograph manuscripts, first editions, and arrangements, scholars have been trying to ascertain the way in which music of the Baroque period may have been performed. The more research that is done, however, the more apparent it becomes that it is impossible to stamp blanket rules over all types of music written throughout Europe during the course of 150 years. In fact, it is even difficult to conclude that certain instructions in a treatise unquestionably reflect the practices of musicians in the specific time and place of the author. For example, as Frederick Neumann points out, J.J. Quantz and C.P.E. Bach, authors of two of the most well-known and often quoted treatises—treatises that totally contradict each other on several points—were both employed by the King of Prussia, Frederick II, at the same time and worked together daily![1] One such contradiction, to be discussed in more detail later, is their respective instructions regarding the execution of dotted rhythms that coexist with triplets. C.P.E. Bach suggests synchronizing the second note of the dotted figure with the third note of the triplet. Quantz, on the other hand, suggests an exaggerated delay of the second note of the dotted figure so as to *avoid* any synchronization.

Certain oral performance traditions or conventions may well have existed, but today we do not have direct access to them. A treatise is simply one person's opinion on the way he or she believes music ought to be performed. It is not a book of rules that all composers and performers of the time subscribed to or were necessarily even aware of. We, as scholars, must be careful not to rely too heavily on the use of Baroque treatises for our research. In fact, Neumann has argued, in "The Use of Baroque Treatises on Musical Performance," that "a treatise is on the whole an undependable source unless it receives decisive support from other quarters."[2] Nevertheless, some 20th century musicologists formulated categorical rules of performance practice based on quotations from Baroque treatises, sometimes citing only one or two references as "proof" of a particular convention.[3]

Musicologists contradicted each other during the 17th and 18th centuries, and they still contradict each other today. At least one point that most "Baroque experts" would have to agree on however, is the fact that in many cases, there are no easy answers. There are some musical situations that can logically be interpreted in more ways than one. The present essay is written with this ambiguity as a fundamental premise.

In this essay, I will offer certain interpretive suggestions for the *Three Sonatas and Three Partitas for Solo Violin* of Johann Sebastian Bach. Two major issues of performance practice will be identified and discussed, with each one being dealt with separately. Historical treatises and 20th century sources will be considered, and in

---

1  Frederick Neumann, "The Dotted Note and the So-Called French Style," *Early Music* 5 (1977): 310-324. Rpt. in Frederick Neumann, *Essays in Performance Practice* (Ann Arbor: UMI Research Press, 1982) 83.

2  Frederick Neumann, "The Use of Baroque Treatises on Musical Performance," *Music and Letters* 48 (1967): 315-324. Rpt. in Neumann, Essays 9.

3  For example, Robert Donington's claim, in *The Interpretation of Early Music* (New York: St. Martin's Press, 1963) 135, that "All Appoggiaturas Take the Beat" (i.e., all appoggiaturas that occur in every piece of music of every composer from every Western-European country writing roughly between the years 1600 and 1750) is supported by just two quotations. The author later qualified this claim to read: "All True Appoggiaturas Take the Beat." See Robert Donington, *The Interpretation of Early Music*, new rev. ed. (New York and London: W.W. Norton, 1989). All subsequent citations of *Interpretation* refer to the 1989 edition.

some cases, with sufficient corroboration, will be used as key pieces of evidence in support of a given solution. However, many conclusions will be arrived at through clues that lie within the music itself. Particular attention will be given to Bach's notation as it appears in the autograph manuscript, a facsimile of which has been used for the preparation of this essay. Many of the ideas presented hereinafter may be applied to other works by Bach and even to other composers of the period. However, it cannot be overstated that blanket rules should be avoided and that each case should be taken individually. Furthermore, a distinction must be made between solo music and ensemble music. Many of the rhythmic alterations that will be discussed, while they may have been utilized by a soloist, could have caused considerable confusion in a 17th or 18th century ensemble, especially when one considers that these groups were generally not directed by a conductor.

Throughout the last two centuries, composers have become more and more specific regarding their instructions to performers; spelling out every precise rhythm, ornament, dynamic, and even rubato, leaving very little to the discretion of the performer. For example, Gustav Mahler would often write complete sentences of expressive indications above certain passages in his orchestral music. This was not the case during the Baroque period. Many pieces were merely skeletal frameworks which the performer was expected to flesh out through realization of the figured bass, ornamentation, added dynamics and articulation, and in some cases, even rhythmic alteration of the printed notes. In fact, this improvisatory performance practice had become so common and so extreme that it led to reactionary comments such as this one written by L'Abbé Laugier in 1754:

> There ought to be a law preventing all singers and all those who make up the orchestra from changing anything in the melody of which the character is traced out for them, with orders to restrict themselves scrupulously to the notation before their eyes. There ought to be a like law obligating all masters who give instruction to instill in their pupils the habit of literal performance.[4]

It should be noted, though, that J.S. Bach is known to have been more complete and precise with his notation than some of his contemporaries. He was actually criticized for cluttering his pages with unnecessary instructions that the contemporary performer would have already understood. In 1737, Johann Adolf Scheibe wrote of Bach:

> All embellishments, all little graces, and all that is understood by the method of playing, he expresses in notes, and not only deprives his pieces of beauty and harmony but makes the melodic line utterly unclear.[5]

We can thus assert that less has to be added to Bach's music than to that of some other Baroque composers, especially in terms of ornamentation. There remain, however, many issues of performance practice that do pertain to Bach which will be discussed presently. This essay will focus on the issues of dotted rhythms and trills. However, brief discussions of vibrato, fingerings, bowing styles, and ritardandos in Baroque music are contained in APPENDICES A, B, C and D respectively.

## **Dotted Rhythms**

Today we understand that the value of a dot is equal to half the value of the note that precedes it. Although this basic formula was also true during the 17th and 18th centuries, there were instances in which a dot's value was intended to mean more than the standard value and, sometimes, less than the standard value (subsequently referred to as *over-dotting* and *under-dotting*). In most cases, the variability of the dot was due to the lack of common usage (although not the lack of existence) of more modern symbols such as the double dot or the quarter-note and eighth-note under a triplet bracket. The *extent* to which composers used the dot to imply values other than the standard is a matter of substantial controversy among musicologists. A brief history of this controversy is necessary for the development of logical interpretations of dotted figures. The first 20th century musicologist to formulate the over-dotting theory was Arnold Dolmetsch. In *The Interpretation of Music of the XVIIth and*

---

4 Abbé Marc-Antoine Laugier, *Apologie de la musique françoise, contre M. Rousseau* (Paris: 1754) 71. Quoted in Donington, Interpretation 156-157.
5 Johann Adolf Scheibe, *Der critische Musicus Hamburg*, (1737-1740). Quoted in Donington, *Interpretation* 155-156.

*XVIIIth Centuries*, first published in 1915, Dolmetsch writes that "exceptions [to the standard value of the dot] were extremely frequent and important."[6] He then goes on to describe and support this theory primarily with quotations from two sources: J.J. Quantz's *Versuch einer Anweisung die Flöte traversiere zu spielen* (1752), and C.P.E. Bach's *Versuch über die wahre Art das Clavier zu spielen*, (first published in 1753).

The famous passages, on which the style of overdotting is fundamentally based, are as follows. Quantz, after describing the standard value of the dot, writes:

> In dotted quavers, semiquavers, and demisemiquavers (see (c), (d), and (e)) you depart from the general rule, because of the animation that those notes express. It is particularly important to observe that the notes after the dots in (c) and (d) must be played just as short as those [after the dots] in (e), whether the tempo is slow or fast.

> EXAMPLE 1: Quantz p. 67.

> As a result, the dotted notes in (c) receive almost the time of a full crotchet, and those in (d) the time of a quaver, since the time of the short notes after the dots cannot actually be fixed with complete exactness...

> ...This rule likewise must be observed when there are triplets in one part and dotted notes against them in the other part. Hence you must not strike the short note after the dot with the third note of the triplet, but after it. Otherwise it will sound like six-eight or twelve-eight time...[7]

> In this metre [alla breve time], as well as in three-four time, the quavers that follow the dotted crotchets in the loure, sarabande, courante, and chaconne must not be played with their literal value, but must be executed in a very short and sharp manner. The dotted note is played with emphasis, and the bow is detached during the dot. All dotted notes are treated in the same manner if time allows; and if three or more demisemiquavers follow a dot or a rest, they are not always played with their literal value, especially in slow pieces, but are executed at the extreme end of the time allotted to them, and with the greatest possible speed, as is frequently the case in overtures, entrées, and furies. Each of these quick notes must receive its separate bow-stroke, and slurring is rarely used.[8]

C.P.E. Bach writes:

> Short notes which follow dotted ones are always shorter in execution than their notated length. Hence it is superfluous to place strokes or dots over them.[9]

> With the advent of an increased use of triplets in common or 4/4 time, as well as in 2/4 and 3/4, many pieces have appeared which might be more conveniently written in 12/8, 9/8, or 6/8. The performance of other lengths against these notes is shown [on p. 65]

---

6    Arnold Dolmetsch, *The Interpretation of Music of the XVIIth and XVIIIth Centuries* (London: Novello, n.d. [1915]) 53.

7    Johann Joachim Quantz, *On Playing the Flute*, trans. Edward R. Reilly (New York: Schirmer Books, 1985) 67-68. See APPENDIX E for the original German text of this and the following quotation taken from the facsimile of J. J. Quantz, *Versuch einer Anweisung die Flöte traversiere zu spielen* (Kassel: Bärenreiter, 1974) 58-59 and 270. All subsequent citations of Quantz refer to the Reilly translation.

8    Quantz 290-291.

9    Carl Philipp Emanuel Bach, *Essay on the True Art of Playing Keyboard Instruments*, trans. and ed. William J. Mitchell (New York: W. W. Norton, 1949) 157. See APPENDIX E for the original German text of this and the following two quotations taken from the facsimile of C.P.E. Bach, *Versuch über die wahre Art das Clavier zu spielen* (Leipzig: C.F. Kahnt, 1906) I: 89-90 and II: 65. All subsequent citations of C.P.E. Bach refer to the Mitchell translation.

[i.e., the note following the dot is to be synchronized *with* the third note of the triplet, not after it].[10]

EXAMPLE 2: C.P.E. Bach p. 160.

Because proper exactness is often lacking in the notation of dotted notes, a general rule of performance has been established which, however, suffers many exceptions. According to this rule, the notes which follow the dots are to be played in the most rapid manner; and often they should be. But sometimes notes in other parts, with which these must enter, are so divided that a modification of the rule is required. Again, a suave affect, which will not survive the essentially defiant character of dotted notes, obliges the performer slightly to shorten the dotted note. Hence, if only one kind of execution is adopted as the basic principle of performance, the other kinds will be lost.[11]

Although Dolmetsch admits that mention of this "conventional lengthening of dots and rests" hadn't been found in any books prior to Quantz's, he dismisses this fact with the statement that double-dots or combined rests equivalent to double-dots were not used until the late 18th century. This is not entirely true. Although certainly not common, double-dots or their equivalent were used earlier by, for example, Chambonnières, Clérambault, Louis Couperin, André Raison, Michel Corrette,[12] and Corelli.[13] Nevertheless, Dolmetsch continues with the assertion that 16th and 17th century music abounds in passages which demand [over-dotting]," and that "we can...feel justified in treating all the old music alike in this respect."[14]

Among the many subsequent musicologists who subscribed to Dolmetsch's theory (at least to some degree), are Thurston Dart and Robert Donington. The former, in *The Interpretation of Music*, first published in 1954, describes the principle of over-dotting and suggests, as an example, that in an overture in the French style, "All dotted rhythms should be adjusted so that they fit the shortest one in the piece; this will often mean that the first note after a rest will need shortening [an 8th-note following an 8th-note rest becoming a 32nd-note following an 8th-note rest and a dotted 16th-note rest] in performance."[15] This implies that if a piece contains dotted 16th/32nd-note figures, then any written dotted quarter-notes should be triple-dotted, making the corresponding 8th-notes 32nd-notes. Dart extends the "convention" of over-dotting from Monteverdi to Beethoven, and warns that "ignorance of this fact is one of the gravest defects of present-day performances of old music."[16] Donington, who studied with Dolmetsch, qualifies the rules of overdotting, saying that when dotted notes are so persistent as to dominate the rhythm or when they form a distinct rhythmic figure or formula, "then it was the convention to crispen them by lengthening the dot, thereby delaying and shortening the note after the dot."[17]

This "convention" of over-dotting apparently went unchallenged until 1965 when Frederick Neumann published "La Note Pointée et la soi-disant 'Manière Française'" in *Revue de Musicologie*, later translated by Raymond Harris and Edmund Shay and republished in *Early Music* (1977) as "The Dotted Note and the So-

---

10 C.P.E. Bach 160.

11 C.P.E. Bach 372.

12 Neumann, "The Dotted Note," *Essays* 85.

13 Donington, *Interpretation* 446.

14 Dolmetsch 62.

15 Thurston Dart, *The Interpretation of Music* (London: Hutchinson, 1962) 81.

16 Dart 81-82.

17 Donington, *Interpretation* 441.

Called French Style."[18] In this article, Neumann cites several musical examples that show (some more convincingly than others) that over-dotting, as condoned by "the style" (Neumann's term for the convention subscribed to by Dolmetsch, Dart, and Donington), does not make sense. He argues that the entire doctrine of over-dotting is based primarily on two sources, the Quantz and C.P.E. Bach essays, which are undeniably contradictory and at best ambiguous. Neumann concludes that the lack of sufficient evidence "suggests that a pronounced and obligatory style of overdotting did not exist."[19] He asserts that the only convention that existed was a greater degree of adaptability in the interpretation of the printed text, including a flexibility towards the relative value of the notes. It was the privilege of the soloist (not so much the ensemble player) to determine whether or not a certain softening or sharpening of the rhythm was demanded by the character of the piece. He or she had to adjust the interpretation of the dot to a given situation, including the question of triplets combined with dotted notes, and that of synchronization. For example, if a dotted quarter/8th-note figure in one voice is set against two dotted 8th/16th-note figures in another voice, should the 8th-note be synchronized with the last 16th-note in the other voice? In any given situation, the performer must choose what he or she deems to be the most musical solution. Moreover, Neumann stresses that "there is a profound and categorical difference between the freedom to lengthen, shorten, or synchronize *according to musical taste*, and a so-called law that would force us to do one or the other.[20]

The controversy over obligatory over-dotting continued for the next two decades with each published article in favor of it, such as those by Michael Collins, David Fuller, John O'Donnell, Graham Pont, and Donington, being systematically argued against by Neumann.[21] It should be noted, however, that while these authors clearly fell on one side of the argument or the other, they were understanding of and open to opposing viewpoints. For example, Donington, in the 1974 edition of *The Interpretation of Early Music*, added a section entitled "Frederick Neumann's Contribution."[22]

Although debates over rhythmic alterations in 17th and 18th century music continue, some more recent scholars seem to have come down in the middle. For instance, Stephen Hefling, who devoted an entire book to the subject, concludes that:

> Overdotting is not a delusion, as Neumann has claimed. But neither is the "French Overture style one of our best-attested conventions of baroque interpretation," as Donington would have it; and Dart's sweeping advocacy of overdotting from Monteverdi through Beethoven extends well beyond what the sources support.[23]

Paul Badura-Skoda, the author of *Interpreting Bach at the Keyboard*, also discusses the controversy and points out that Neumann "is now willing on occasion to admit the validity of double dotting."[24] This is actually a misleading comment, for in his very first article on the subject ("The Dotted Note..."), Neumann acknowledges the flexibility of the dot and even cites an example where double-dotting is appropriate.[25]

---

18 Neumann, "The Dotted Note," *Essays* 73-98.

19 Neumann, "The Dotted Note," *Essays* 98.

20 Neumann, "The Dotted Note," *Essays* 94.

21 Michael Collins, "A Reconsideration of French Over-Dotting," *Music and Letters* (1969): 111-123. David Fuller, "Dotting, the 'French Style' and Frederick Neumann's Counter-Reformation," *Early Music* 5 (1977): 517. John O'Donnell, "The French Style and the Overtures of Bach," *Early Music* 7 (1979): 190 and 336. Graham Pont, "French Overtures at the Keyboard: How Handel Rendered the Playing of Them," *Musicology* 6 (1980): 29. Donington, *Interpretation* 451. Frederick Neumann, "Rhythm in the Two Versions of Bach's French Overture, BWV 831," *Studies in Renaissance and Baroque Music in Honor of Arthur Mendel*, (Kassel, 1974): 183-194. Rpt. in *Essays* 99-110. Frederick Neumann, "Facts and Fiction about Overdotting," *The Musical Quarterly* 63 (1977): 155-185. Rpt. in *Essays* 111-133. Frederick Neumann, "Once More: The 'French Overture Style,'" *Early Music* 7 (1979): 39-45. Rpt. in *Essays* 137-150. Frederick Neumann, "The Overdotting Syndrome: Anatomy of a Delusion," *The Musical Quarterly* 67 (1981): 305-347. Rpt. in *Essays* 151-182.

22 Donington, *Interpretation* 620.

23 Stephen E. Hefling, *Rhythmic Alteration in Seventeenth- and Eighteenth-Century Music: Notes Inégales and Overdotting* (New York: Schirmer Books, 1993) 145.

24 Paul Badura-Skoda, *Interpreting Bach at the Keyboard*, trans. Alfred Clayton (Oxford: Clarendon Press, 1993) 56.

25 In Neumann, "The Dotted Note," *Essays* 94, the author describes a scenario in which the 8th-note of a dotted quarter/8th-note figure should be synchronized with the 16th-note of a dotted 8th/16th-note figure (i.e., the dotted quarter should be double-dotted) because failure to do so would disrupt the otherwise consistent flow of parallel sixths. (The example, number 32, appears on page 92 but is discussed on page 94).

The above discussion makes it clear that there is not one easy answer to the question of dotted rhythms in Baroque music. Therefore, blanket rules should be avoided, and each case must be taken individually. When making decisions about the execution of dotted figures, clues can often be found in the relationship between voices. However, in primarily melodic contexts, where there are no other voices with which to compare, the clues are much less apparent. Decisions become significantly more difficult and even somewhat arbitrary. It is imperative that one keep this frame of mind while analyzing the following suggestions.

**Sonata No. 1 in g minor**

<u>Adagio</u>: This movement contains three kinds of dotted figures: dotted 32nds, dotted 16ths, and one dotted 8th. The dotted 32nd/64th-note figure in m. 8 need not be over-dotted for two reasons. First, its inherent quickness does not allow for any further sharpening; and second, it is the shortest dotted figure in the piece. Even the strongest supporters of obligatory over-dotting profess that it is the shortest dotted figure in the piece to which the *others* are adjusted to fit.[26] However, the dotted 32nd/64th-note figure in m. 21 may be treated freely within the ritardando that could be applied before the final chord.[27]

The way a figure is notated in relation to the notes which surround it can often be a telling factor as to the intended execution. In each of the dotted 16th/32nd-note figures in mm. 6, 11, 16/b. 3 (beat 3),[28] 19, and 21/b. 3, the 32nd-note that follows the dotted 16th is beamed together with the ensuing 32nd-notes, implying that all are of equal value and that the figure should therefore be executed literally. The same reasoning can be applied to cases in which two 64th-notes (instead of one 32nd-note) follow a dotted 16th and are beamed together with the ensuing 32nd-notes. Such is the case in both mm. 10/b. 4 and 14/b. 1. It must be pointed out, however, that Bach sometimes notated dotted figures that made for mathematical impossibilities. See, for example, m. 21/b. 2. As shown below, the autograph manuscript contains a dotted 16th followed by three 64th-notes.

EXAMPLE 3: Sonata No.1, Adagio mm. 20-21.

It is explained in both the *Bach-Gesellschaft* edition and the *Neue Bach-Ausgabe* that Bach often used a dotted note followed by three short notes, e.g. ♩. ♫, interchangeably with (and as shorthand for) the more precise notation of an un-dotted note tied to the first of four short notes ♩♫♫.[29] This fact is also agreed upon by many modern scholars and is supported by several primary sources.[30] The present edition of Bach's sonatas and partitas has replaced each case of a mathematically impossible dotted rhythm with the more precise tied notation.

The two dotted 16th/32nd-note figures in m. 20 should probably be played as written, in keeping with the aforementioned figures of equal value. However, care should be taken not to *under*-dot them, so as to accentuate the variation between this measure and beat 1 of m. 7. The four remaining dotted 16th/32nd-note figures in this movement are similar to numerous other examples in Bach's works as well as those of virtually every other composer. Specifically, the short note or notes that follow the dot are *ornamental in character*. They could take the form of anticipations, neighbor or auxiliary tones, escape tones, passing tones, and especially after trills (where the principal note is trilled during the dotted note), *Nachschläge* [after-beats].[31] Even Frederick

---

26 Dart 81.

27 See APPENDIX D for a brief discussion of ritardandos in Baroque music.

28 The beat of a given figure will only be specified if there are two or more of the same type in one measure. In such cases, the beat referred to will be the one implied by the time signature, regardless of tempo. For example, in this movement, the beat referred to is that of a quarter-note, even if some performers might think of the movement "in 8."

29 Neumann, "Facts and Fiction," *Essays* 293, note 38.

30 See, for example, Hefling 67. The author cites Sperling, Schmelz, Titelouze, Loulié, and Metoyen as primary sources. Neumann, in "Facts and Fiction, "*Essays* 122, also cites Sperling and Schmelz.

31 For further explanation of these ornaments see, for example, Don Randel, ed.. *The New Harvard Dictionary of Music* (Cambridge, MA and London: Harvard University Press, 1986) 205-206 and 525.

Neumann, the leader of the "Counter-Reformation" against obligatory over-dotting, suggests that when dots are followed by one or more notes that are ornamental in character yet written as regular sized notes (i.e., not small, unmeasured pitches), those notes often can be played faster and/or lighter than the surrounding structural pitches, consequently lengthening the preceding dot. He emphasizes the fact that it is the shortening of the ornamental notes that leads to over-dotting, not vice versa.[32] Let it be understood that any suggestion to treat a note or notes ornamentally does not necessarily imply that they should be played as quickly as possible, especially at important cadences where ritardandos might be added. The ornaments simply should not be given the weight and emphasis that structural notes receive. With this being said, the 32nd-notes (or two 64th-notes) that follow dotted 16ths in mm. 2, 5, 12, and 16/b. 4 are ornamental in character and should be treated as such. The one dotted 8th/16-note figure in this movement appears in m. 8. Although the 16th-note is ornamental in character, it should probably not be played too quickly in that it occurs at the important dominant cadence during which a slight ritardando may be applied.

Fuga; Allegro: The dotted 8th/16-note figures here are the shortest dotted rhythms in the movement and are already quick enough to negate the need for rhythmic alteration. However, several of them—namely those in mm. 24, 54, 86, and 94—could be treated ornamentally in terms of giving less emphasis to the 16th-notes. In m. 35, the dotted 8th/16-note figure is accompanied by two even 8th-notes in the lower voice. This rhythmic variety should be presented clearly (i.e., quite literally) because in a fugue, the independence of the voices and the way they interact is of fundamental importance. The dotted quarter-note in m. 93 is part of a recitative-like passage that could be taken freely and out of tempo.

Siciliana: In this movement, several factors point to the literal execution of the dotted 8th/16-note figures. First and most importantly, the character of the movement is one of repose, an indication that crisp dotted rhythms do not belong. In addition, these figures are the only (and therefore the shortest) in the movement. Finally, the moving 16th-notes that accompany the dotted figure in m. 2 preclude any rhythmic alterations.

**Partita No. 1 in b minor**

Allemanda: Although dotted notes were extremely common during Bach's lifetime, dotted *rests* were practically never used. If a composer wanted to notate, for example, the equivalent of a dotted 8th worth of silence, he or she would write an 8th-note rest followed by a 16th-note rest. In fact, Badura-Skoda writes that the "practice of dotting rests was unknown in the Baroque era, and only gradually came into use after about 1750." He goes on to say that "some readers may object" that Bach did occasionally use dotted rests. Badura-Skoda insists, however, that there are no dotted rests in Bach's autograph manuscripts and that any such example found is actually a modern editor's alteration.[33] With all due respect for Mr. Badura-Skoda, I must object. In m. 4 of this movement (the Allemanda of Partita No.1 in b minor for Solo Violin), Bach's *autograph manuscript* contains two dotted 16th-note rests!

In any event, with the exception of its final chord, this movement contains two kinds of dotted figures, namely dotted 16ths and dotted 8ths. The former need not be over-dotted for two reasons. First, their inherent quickness does not allow for any further sharpening; and second, they are the shortest dotted figures in the piece. Therefore, the only ones in question are the dotted 8ths. Donington describes a situation calling for over-dotting in which the dotted figures are so persistent as to dominate the rhythm.[34] He cites as source material a passage from Reichhardt which reads: "When [notes] are dotted one after the other, the shorter notes should be taken as short as possible to give more emphasis to the longer."[35] Furthermore, in her recent book, *Performing Baroque Music*, Mary Cyr lists pieces which are slow, noble, stately, march-like, or vigorous as likely to be considered for over-dotting.[36] This is supported by statements from Quantz, C.P.E. Bach, and Leopold Mozart. For example, the latter, in his 1756 treatise, wrote:

---

32 Neumann, "Facts and Fiction," *Essays* 124.
33 Badura-Skoda 50-51.
34 Donington, *Interpretation* 441.
35 Johann Friedrich Reichhardt, *Über die Phlichten des Ripien-Violinisten* (Berlin and Leipzig: 1776) Sect. ii. Quoted in Donington, *Interpretation* 444.
36 Mary Cyr, *Performing Baroque Music* (Portland, OR: Amadeus Press, 1992) 119.

> There are certain passages in slow pieces where the dot must be held rather longer than the afore-mentioned rule demands if the performance is not to sound too sleepy…In such cases dotted notes must be held somewhat longer, but the time taken up by the extended value must be, so to speak, stolen from the note standing after the dot.[37]

The b minor Allemanda definitely qualifies as a piece in which dotted figures dominate the rhythm, and it certainly can be characterized as slow, noble, and stately. Nevertheless, in accordance with the present goal, each case will be looked at individually.

A fairly strong argument can be made for overdotting at least 14 of the 15 dotted 8th/16th-note figures in the movement. Each of the 16th-notes (or two 32nd-notes) following dotted 8ths occurring in the first two measures are ornamental and could be played faster and lighter than notated. This principle also applies to each dotted 8th/16th-note figure found in mm. 8, 9, 11, 12, 16, 18, 19, and 24. If over-dotting is applied to these measures, then the pick-up to both mm. 1 and 13 should be delayed as well (answering the question of the dotted quarter in m. 24).

Among these dotted 8th/16-note figures, those which are followed by triplets raise additional questions. For example, in m. 16, should the 16th-note that follows the dotted 8th be delayed to the extent of making it a 16th-note triplet, hence conforming to the following triplets, or should the dotted 8th be exactly double-dotted in order to clearly delineate its duple nature from the following triplets? Because the former solution would, in both mm. 16 and 19, neatly divide the measures in half between duples and triplets, it is arguably the better choice.

There remain two dotted 8ths whose corresponding 16th-notes are not simply ornamental in character. The one in m. 3 could be exactly double-dotted in order to make the next note conform to the succeeding sequence of 32nd-note pick-ups. Finally, the dotted 8th in m. 14, although ambiguous, could also be double-dotted to make the next note conform to the following 32nds, and to be consistent with the interpretation of the rest of the movement.

Double: The dotted 8ths that end each section (mm. 12 and 24 respectively) should be played literally so that the following pick-ups fit in with the continual flow of 16th-notes.

Corrente: Similarly, the dotted quarter that ends the first section (m. 32) should be played literally so that the following pick-up fits in with the continual flow of 8th-notes.

Double; Presto: Again, the dotted 8ths that end each section (mm. 32 and 80 respectively) should be played literally so that the following pick-ups fit in with the continual flow of 16th-notes.

Sarabande: The dotted quarter/8th-note figures in this movement pose an interesting question. According to Quantz, the 8th-notes that follow dotted quarters in a sarabande "must not be played with their literal value, but must be executed in a very short and sharp manner."[38] Dolmetsch and his followers have interpreted this statement as an instruction to over-dot the dotted quarters and delay the 8th-notes. Neumann, on the other hand, contends that (even if this one source were reason enough to overdot the dotted quarters) Quantz was not implying that at all. Neumann interprets the passage as implying that the dotted quarters are not over-dotted, but that the 8th-notes are given less than their literal value (i.e., the 8th-notes begin at their notated time, but are played short).[39] Regardless of what Quantz meant, there is internal evidence that precludes rhythmic alteration of the dotted quarters in this movement. In m. 13, the note following the dotted quarter is clearly aligned with the fourth of four accompanying 8th-notes and should undoubtedly be synchronized with it. Furthermore, the beaming together of the three 8th-notes following dotted quarters in mm. 2, 4, 8, 12, 16, and 24 suggest equal 8th-notes and subsequently standard dotted quarters.

---

37 Leopold Mozart, *A Treatise on the Fundamental Principles of Violin Playing* (1756), trans. Editha Knocker (London and New York: Oxford University Press, 1972) 5th imp. 41.

38 Quantz 290.

39 Neumann, "The Overdotting Syndrome," *Essays* 172-173.

Tempo di Borea: It is almost unnecessary to discuss the dotted half-notes in this movement because no primary or secondary sources suggest their prolongation. Even if one did, there is ample internal evidence to discredit such a suggestion. For example, the note following the dotted half in m. 28 is clearly aligned with the fourth of four accompanying quarter-notes and should undoubtedly be synchronized with it.

**Sonata No. 2 in a minor**

Grave: This movement contains three kinds of dotted figures: dotted 32nds, dotted 16ths, and dotted 8ths. The dotted 32nd/64th-note figures in mm. 4 and 19 need not be over-dotted for two reasons. First, their inherent quickness does not allow for any further sharpening; and second, they are the shortest dotted figures in the piece.

The beaming together of the 32nd-notes following dotted 16ths in mm. 2/b. 4, 7/b. 4, and 15/b. 3 makes it quite clear that these dotted rhythms were intended to be performed literally. For the sake of consistency, I would suggest that all other dotted 16ths in this movement be played literally as well. However, the 32nd-note and the two 64th-notes at the end of beat 2 in mm. 16 and 18 respectively are cadential *Nachschläge* and should be treated ornamentally.

Of the thirteen dotted 8ths in the movement, seven have corresponding short notes that are ornamental in character and should be treated as such. They occur in mm. 3, 4/b. 4, 6, 8/b. 2 & 3, and 11/b. 3 & 4. The figures in both mm. 10 and 20/b. 1 are directly followed by four 16th-notes, making a literal 16th-note pick-up to the group of four logical. Similarly, it follows that the eight 32nd-notes in m. 20/b. 4 should be preceded by two literal 32nds. The 16th-note that follows the dotted 8th in m. 21 could be interpreted as being part of the short sequence that occurs over the next two beats. Since the second segment of the pattern, beat 4, is preceded by a 16th-note, the first segment, beat 3, should be approached the same way, i.e., by a literal 16th-note.

The two remaining dotted 8th/16th-note figures occur in mm. 4/b. 1 and 5. The latter could be played in the same manner as that suggested for mm. 16 and 19 in the Allemanda of Partita No.1. In other words, delaying the 16th-note to the extent of making it a 16th-note triplet, hence conforming to the following triplets. However, because there are no apparent clues one way or the other, and because this movement contains a mixture of literal and over-dotted figures, the dotted 8th/16th-note in m. 4/b. 1 should probably be played as written.

Fuga: The dotted 8th/16-note figures here are the shortest dotted rhythms in the movement and are already quick enough to negate the need for rhythmic alteration. Furthermore, in mm. 44, 136, 165, and 279 the first dotted 8th/16-note figure is accompanied by two even 8th-notes in the lower voice. This rhythmic variety should be presented clearly (i.e., quite literally) because in a fugue, the independence of the voices and the way they interact is of fundamental importance. Literal execution of the dotted 8th/16th-notes in this movement is also evidenced by the figure in m. 260. The 16th-note that follows the dotted 8th is the first note of a two measure sequence consisting solely of consecutive 16th-notes. Any rhythmic alterations would disrupt the intended flow.

The only other dotted figure in the movement is that which occurs in m. 177. The 8th-note following the dotted quarter is part of a four measure flow of steady 8th-notes which should not be disrupted by altering the dotted quarter.

Andante: This movement contains only two dotted rhythms, both of which occur in m. 25.[40] The beaming together of the 32nd-notes following the dotted 16th make their equal value clear and indicate literal execution. However, the two 32-notes at the end of beat 3 should be treated ornamentally. They could be slightly more elongated on the repeat, though, where a ritardando may be applied.

**Partita No. 2 in d minor**

Allemanda: All dotted figures in this movement should be executed literally so as not to disrupt the steady flow of 16th-notes. Likewise, both the pick-up to m. 1 and to m. 17 should be exact 16th-notes.

---

[40] There are two dotted half-notes in this movement, but they each constitute a full measure and therefore do not have corresponding quarter-notes to qualify them as "dotted figures". Throughout the essay, dotted notes such as these will not be discussed.

Corrente: In this movement, Bach ostensibly juxtaposes triplets and dotted 8th/16th-note figures. However, because the quarter-eighth under a triplet bracket was virtually unused by Bach or his contemporaries, I believe that in this case, he used the dotted figure to indicate a 2:1 ratio of under-dotting.[41] This is one of those pieces that, according to C.P.E. Bach, "might be more conveniently written in 12/8, 9/8, or 6/8."[42] Several modern scholars support this theory. In *Performing Baroque Music*, Cyr describes the inexact notation, cites several examples, and stresses that it is important to express a single character or affect by resolving any notational conflicts.[43] Badura-Skoda agrees, recommending that in the majority of passages in Bach where dotted rhythms coincide with triplets, they should be assimilated to the triplets as suggested by C.P.E. Bach.[44] However, this sentiment is by no means universal. As previously shown, Quantz would place the 16th-note *after* the third triplet, not with it. In addition, Johann Friedrich Agricola, who studied with J.S. Bach, claimed that his teacher instructed pupils to execute dotted rhythms beneath triplets precisely as notated.[45]

Perhaps the most convincing argument regarding the triplet problem comes from Neumann. In "Facts and Fiction About Overdotting," he presents several musical examples that make it virtually impossible to deny that Bach, at least in the given examples, used dotted figures to denote a 2:1 triplet rhythm. For instance, Neumann shows that the autograph score's continuo part of Cantata No. 94 is written in 12/8 with a quarter-eighth 2:1 ratio, while the corresponding measures in the autograph organ part appear in dotted rhythms![46]

EXAMPLE 4: Bach Cantata No. 94, mm. 70-71.

Although it is obviously debatable, I believe that in the case of the Corrente from Partita No. 2, Bach used dotted figures to indicate a 2:1 ratio and that the dotted 8th/16th-notes should be under-dotted accordingly. In keeping with this interpretation, the 16th-note pick-up to both mm. 1 and 25 should be treated like the third note of a triplet.

Sarabanda: This movement contains three kinds of dotted figures: dotted 16ths, dotted 8ths, and dotted quarters. The dotted 16th/32nd-note figure in m. 4 need not be over-dotted for three reasons. First, its inherent quickness does not allow for any further sharpening; second, it is the shortest dotted figure in the piece; and third, the 32nd-note that follows the dotted 16th is beamed together with the ensuing 32nd-notes, implying that all are of equal value and that the figure should therefore be executed literally. The first two reasons apply to the dotted 16th/32nd-note figure in m. 19 as well.

While the two 32nd-notes following the dotted 8th in both mm. 9 and 25 should be considered ornamental, the 16th-notes that follow the other dotted 8ths in the movement, namely those in mm. 17, 18, and 24, are more structural in nature. Furthermore, the figures in mm. 17 and 24 are embedded in descending scales made up primarily of 16th-notes, suggesting against any rhythmic alteration.

---

41 Neumann points out, in "Facts and Fiction," *Essays* 293, note 35, that there are at least two instances in which Bach used the quarter-eighth under a triplet bracket. This notation appears in the autographs of Cantata No. 105 (mm. 18-19 of the final chorale) and of the Orgelbüchlein in "In dulci jubilo" (mm. 25-26). Neumann stresses, however, that these "are insignificant exceptions to the infinite mass of dotted notes with 2:1 meaning."

42 C.P.E. Bach 160.

43 Cyr 119.

44 Badura-Skoda 44.

45 Hans Joachim Schulze, ed., *Bach-Dokumente: Fremdschriftliche und gedruckte Dokumente zur Lebensgeschichte Johann Sebastian Bachs 1685-1750* (Kassel and Leipzig, 1969) 206. Cited in Badura-Skoda 41-42.

46 Neumann, "Facts and Fiction," *Essays* 121-122. The author attributes this example to Walter Emery.

Just as they did in the Sarabande of Partita No.1, the dotted quarter/8th-note figures in this movement pose some interesting questions. 1) Was Quantz's directive regarding dotted quarter/8th-note figures in French dances an implication of over-dotting or merely one of articulation? 2) If Quantz was implying over-dotting, is this one source reason enough to do it? And 3) does Bach's use of the *Italian* spelling of Sarabanda for this movement (as opposed to the French Sarabande) make the whole matter moot?[47] Once again, the answers must be searched for within the music itself. Unfortunately, Bach does not give us any obvious clues in this case. With so much doubt and contradiction surrounding the matter, it is probably wisest simply to play the rhythm more or less as Bach notated it. However, the dotted quarters on beat 2 of mm. 1, 2, 6, 9, and 25 should probably be stressed, as this is characteristic of the Sarabanda. This stress may lead to a *slight* prolongation of the dotted quarters and a subsequent shortening and reduction in weight of the following 8th-notes.

Ciaccona: This movement is similar to the previous one discussed in that it highlights the "sarabande syncopation module" of a stressed second beat.[48] In addition, it raises the same three unanswerable questions. As in the Sarabanda, clues within the music are our only real guide. However, unlike the Sarabanda, this movement *does* contain internal evidence that supports more or less literal execution, and perhaps even precludes any prolongation of the dotted quarters whatsoever. As Neumann points out in "Facts and Fiction About Overdotting," there are several instances, namely mm. 137-146 and mm. 178-200, where the dotted quarter/8th-note theme is accompanied by moving 8th-notes, making any rhythmic alteration impossible.[49] In retrospect, the opening theme, even though there are no moving 8th-notes to restrict it, should therefore be played as notated.

For the sake of argument, it should be mentioned that in the second variation, mm. 17-24, a rhythmic figure recurs which consists of two quarter-notes followed by an 8th-note rest, a 16th-note rest, and a 16th-note—in other words, the equivalent of a quarter-note followed by a *double*-dotted quarter and a 16th-note. One could conceivably argue that this is an indication that the opening theme should be double-dotted.[50] However, the above evidence for literal execution is much more prevalent and far more convincing. If the opening were overdotted, then the main theme of the movement would wind up being played with different rhythms at various points in the piece. It is unlikely that this was Bach's intention.

The only other dotted figures in the movement are dotted 8th/16th-notes. In mm. 8-24, the dotted figures completely dominate the rhythm, appearing on all but one beat for sixteen and two-thirds consecutive measures. For this reason, the dotted figures should be emphasized by crisp, sharp articulation. As Donington points out though, this does not necessarily mean that they should be *double*-dotted.[51] Contrarily, the dotted 8ths in mm. 210-216 should be executed quite literally because of their corresponding 16th-notes' obvious connection to the ensuing 16th-note passages.

**Sonata No. 3 in C Major**

Adagio: This movement contains three kinds of dotted figures: dotted 16ths, dotted 8ths, and dotted quarters. The dotted 16th/32nd-note figures in mm. 12 and 39 need not be over-dotted for three reasons. First, their inherent quickness does not allow for any further sharpening; second, they are the shortest dotted figures in the piece; and third, the 32nd-note that follows the dotted 16th in both cases is beamed together with the ensuing 32nd-notes, implying that all are of equal value and that the figures should therefore be executed literally. Additionally, there is nothing to indicate that either of the two dotted quarter/8th-note figures, in mm. 11 and 38 respectively, should be rhythmically altered.

The most controversial figures in this movement are the dotted 8th/16th-notes. There is no question that these dotted figures dominate the rhythm, which according to Donington, makes them prime candidates for over-dot-

---

47  For movement titles, Bach uses all Italian spellings except for the Sarabande in Partita #1, all Italian spellings in Partita #2, and all French spellings in Partita #3.

48  Meredith Little and Natalie Jenne, *Dance and the Music of J.S. Bach* (Bloomington and Indianapolis: Indiana University Press, 1991) 203.

49  Neumann, "Facts and Fiction," *Essays* 118.

50  Hear, for example, J.S. Bach, Sonatas and Partitas: BWV 1001-1006, Sigiswald Kuijken, Violin, Editio Classica, 77043-2-RG, 1990, Disc 2: track 5.

51  Donington, *Interpretation* 441.

ting. Some violinists do, in fact, perform this movement with over-dotted 8ths.[52] However, while it is definitely slow, this piece is certainly not noble, stately, march-like, or vigorous. It is more gentle, flowing, and elegant—a movement that Cyr would call "fundamentally different in character" from pieces in which over-dotting applies.[53]

I feel that the most important consideration in performing these figures is that the dotted 8ths are the main notes, and the 16th-notes are ornamental neighbor tones. However, considerable delaying of the 16th-notes would sound a bit choppy for this essentially legato movement. Therefore, I would suggest playing the dotted 8th/16th-note figures more or less as notated, but with less emphasis given to the 16th-notes. Tempo, though, is an important factor here (and in many other cases as well). If the movement is taken extremely slowly, then the 16th-notes should be delayed enough so that they do not sound labored.

Fuga: Because the dotted quarter/8th-note figures in mm. 163 and 244 are the only dotted rhythms (and therefore the shortest) in the movement, and because the predominant flow is that of 8th-notes, they need not be over-dotted.

Largo: The dotted 16th/32nd-note figures in mm. 13, 14, 19, and 20 need not be over-dotted for three reasons. First, their inherent quickness does not allow for any further sharpening; second, they are the shortest dotted figures in the piece; and third, the 32nd-note that follows the dotted 16th in all cases is beamed together with the ensuing 32nd-notes, implying that all are of equal value and that the figures should therefore be executed literally. Furthermore, the dotted 8th/16th-note figures in mm. 7 and 17 are bound by the continuous flow of 16th-notes in which they are embedded and therefore should also be played precisely as notated. However, the figure in m. 21 could be treated freely within the ritardando that may be applied before the final chord.

## Partita No. 3 in E Major

Preludio: The only dotted rhythms of any kind in this movement are the dotted quarter/8th-note figures that appear in mm. 134 and 135. The whole point of these two measures is to contrast the preceding one hundred and thirty-one measures of consecutive 16th-notes. Although it is true that both 8th-notes in these two measures could be considered ornamental in character, any shortening or de-emphasis of them, through over-dotting, would take away from the intended effect. Therefore, both 8th-notes should probably be given their full value (even if a ritenuto is employed), as well as a certain amount of emphasis.

Loure: Of the thirty-two movements that make up Bach's unaccompanied violin works, this is perhaps the most difficult to interpret in terms of the over-dotting question. There is not only substantial scholarly backing, but internal evidence for both literal execution *and* over-dotting of the dotted quarter/8th-note figures in this piece. A striking characteristic of most loures is the *saultillant* rhythm: dotted quarter/8th-note/quarter-note, which is often used almost continually.[54] In this movement, the pattern often begins in the middle (i.e., on the 8th-note), and it is the execution of this rhythm that causes much confusion.

The argument for literal execution is based on three observations. First, the two even 8th-notes that accompany the *saultillant* rhythm in m. 12 ostensibly preclude over-dotting in that measure. Second, the 8th-note embellishing figures that precede the *saultillant* rhythm at the end of mm. 4, 8, 13, and 21 indicate that real 8th-notes are an integral component of the rhythm in question. Finally, Little and Jenne's discussion in *Dance and the Music of J. S. Bach* about the connection between the loure and the French gigue exposes an important piece of information. They explain that the slow tempo of the loure gives it a more languid quality than the energetic gigue. Further, this languid quality is created in part "by the almost hypnotic repetition of the *slow-moving* 'saultillant' rhythm."[55] [Italics mine]

---

52 Hear, for example, Kuijken Disc 2: track 6.
53 Cyr 119.
54 Little and Jenne 186.
55 Little and Jenne 186.

Equally convincing arguments can be made for an over-dotted execution of the *saultillant* rhythm. The presentation of the theme in mm. 4, 6, 7, 10, 17, 19, and 22 contains a 16th-note in between the implied dotted quarter and quarter-note. This is brought about by a quarter-note tied to a dotted 8th/16th-note figure in each half measure. If Bach had wanted to maintain the *saultillant* rhythm consisting of a real 8th-note in between the implied dotted quarter and quarter-note, why did he not tie the quarter-note to the first of two even 8th-notes instead of to the dotted 8th/16th-note figure? This may be an indication that Bach intended all occurrences of the theme to include a 16th-note instead of an 8th-note, but simply could not notate them as such due to the unavailability (i.e., lack of common usage) of the double-dot. In any case, these measures at least indicate that 16th-notes are *also* an integral part of the rhythm in question.

Scholarly sources, both primary and secondary, point to the over-dotted rendition of the loure's *saultillant* rhythm. Discarding Quantz's directive for its ambiguity, an explicit instruction for performance of the loure's characteristic rhythm appears in the entry for "loure" in *Allgemeine Theorie der schönen Künste* of 1771. The article, apparently written by Johann Philipp Kirnberger and J.A.P. Schulz (it may have been written by Schulz alone), includes the following statement:

> Um den Einschnitt nach dem ersten punktirten Viertel jedes Takts im Vortrag fühlbar zu machen, muß auf der Violin die Achtelnote wie ein Sechszehntheil hinauf, die darauf folgenden zwey Viertel aber stark herunter gestrichen und besonders das punktirte Viertel schweer angehalten werden.
>
> In order to make the [caesura] after the first dotted quarter of each beat palpable in performance, on the violin the eighth note has to be like a sixteenth, upbow, but the following two quarters are strongly stroked downbow, and in particular the dotted quarter must be arduously sustained.[56]

Admittedly, this is a fairly late source in terms of relevance to J.S. Bach and it is probably more applicable to the then modern galant style. In fact, one of Neumann's chief arguments against using sources such as Quantz and C.P.E. Bach is that they are essentially composers in the galant style, for which over-dotting was an essential element.[57] However, according to Christoph Wolff, the Loure, Gavotte en Rondeaux, and Menuet of this Partita *are* "galant pieces in a more modern style,"[58] making J.S. Bach's progressiveness a factor pointing towards an over-dotted rendition of this movement.

Although it is unquestionably debatable, it appears that the arguments for over-dotting the *saultillant* rhythm, especially the internal evidence, are stronger than those for literal execution. As for the dotted 8th/16th-note figures in this movement, more or less literal execution seems obvious from the above discussion. However, the 16th-notes in these figures, as well as the delayed 8th-notes following over-dotted quarters, should not be played so crisply as to destroy the movement's languid character.

<u>Gavotte en Rondeaux:</u> This movement contains two dotted figures, both of them dotted quarter/8th-notes, that occur in mm. 39 and 63 respectively. Because of the general flow of 8th-notes and the virtual lack of 16th-notes in the piece, both figures should be played as notated.

<u>Menuet I:</u> The only dotted figure of this movement is the dotted quarter in m. 18. The continual 3+3 pattern of 8th-notes in mm. 19-26 makes the literal execution of the dotted quarter in m. 18 obvious.

<u>Gigue:</u> The continuous flow of 16th-notes surrounding the lone dotted figure of the movement, the dotted 8th in m. 4, precludes any rhythmic alteration of it.

---

56 Johann Philipp Kirnberger and J.A.P. Schulz, *Allgemeine Theorie der schönen Künste* (1771) 2: 722: "Loure." Quoted in Hefling 115.

57 Neumann, "Facts and Fiction," *Essays* 129.

58 Christoph Wolff, liner notes, J.S. Bach, Sonatas and Partitas: BWV 1001-1006, Sigiswald Kuijken, Violin, Editio Classica, 77043-2-RG, 1990.

# Trills

A trill, by definition, is the alternation between a written (principal or main) note and the pitch directly above it, the auxiliary note. The upper note is the next pitch above the principal note within the key, unless otherwise indicated by an accidental above the trill sign or one earlier in the measure. However, there are several other aspects to any given trill which are usually not specified by the composer and must be interpreted by the performer based on the historical and musical context of the piece. These aspects include which of the two pitches is sounded first, and whether that pitch is played on the beat or before the beat. The interpretation of trills in Baroque music is not as highly debated as the issue of over-dotting, although there is considerable disagreement. The modern "doctrine" or "rule" is that all trills in Baroque music begin with the auxiliary note—on the beat. Some who adhere to this rule do allow for rare exceptions while others allow for none. Neumann, on the other hand, feels that there are many allowable ways of performing trills. He does agree, however, that the upper note start should be given first consideration. In his article entitled "Misconceptions about the French Trill in the 17th and 18th Centuries," he writes: "it was during Bach's lifetime that in Germany the former [Italo-German] preference for the start with the main note gradually gave way to one with the upper note [as per French influences], it is very probable that the upper-note start, *on or before* the beat, ought to be given first consideration."[59]

The modern rule of starting the Baroque trill with the upper note is derived from a number of historical sources. For instance, J.M. Hotteterre wrote in 1707 that "[trills begin] on the sound above..."[60] Quantz wrote that "each shake begins with the appoggiatura that precedes its note..."[61] In 1756 Marpurg agreed, stating that "the trill...starts on the accessory note."[62] One of the most authoritative and unambiguous directives comes from François Couperin. In his *Méthode*, he writes that "on whatever note a shake may be marked, one must always begin it on the whole-tone or half-tone above."[63]

The "on-the-beat" portion of the rule owes its existence primarily to ornamentation tables of the period. Several treatises, such as those by Playford, Purcell, D'Anglebert, Couperin, and C.P.E. Bach, showed trill signs and their execution—generally with the trills beginning on the beat.[64] Even J.S. Bach himself presented an ornamentation table, with the upper note/on-the-beat trill, in the elementary musical instruction book that he wrote for his son known as the *Wilhelm Friedmann Büchlein*.[65]

Some modern proponents of this rule are more strict about it than others. Dolmetsch, after describing the upper note/on-the-beat trill, claims that it is entirely applicable to Bach and that "it is impossible...to justify any exception about the execution of shakes or other ornaments in his music."[66] Putnam Aldrich writes that "it is certain, not because of any rule, but by definition, that the trill always begins with the note above the main note."[67] Furthermore, in *Ornamentation in J. S. Bach's Organ Works*, Aldrich states that "there are *no* exceptions, in Bach's music, to the rule that *the trill begins with the note above the written note*.[68] Equally dogmatic, Ralph Kirkpatrick stresses that "it cannot be too emphatically stated that the Bach trill always begins with the upper note..."[69]

---

59 Frederick Neumann, "Misconceptions About the French Trill in the 17th and 18th Centuries," *The Musical Quarterly* 50 (1964): 188-206. Rpt. in Neumann, *Essays* 196.

60 J.M. Hotteterre, *Principes de la flûte traversière* (Paris: 1707) 11. Quoted in Donington, *Interpretation* 243.

61 Quantz 103.

62 F.W. Marpurg, *Principes du clavecin* (Berlin: 1756) 66. Quoted in Donington, *Interpretation* 244.

63 Quoted in Dolmetsch 166.

64 Donington, *Interpretation* 242-245.

65 This ornamentation table is contained in Rosalyn Tureck, *An Introduction to the Performance of Bach* (London: Oxford University Press, 1960) II: 9.

66 Dolmetsch 168.

67 Putnam Aldrich, "On the Interpretation of Bach's Trills," *The Musical Quarterly* 49 (1963): 298.

68 Putnam Aldrich, *Ornamentation in J.S. Bach's Organ Works* (New York: Coleman-Ross, 1950) 32.

69 Ralph Kirkpatrick, ed., J.S. Bach, *Goldberg Variations* (New York: 1938) xiii-xiv. Quoted in Frederick Neumann, *Ornamentation in Baroque and Post-Baroque Music: With Special Emphasis on J.S. Bach* (Princeton: Princeton University Press, 1978) 312-313.

Among the more liberal was Edward Dannreuther, who listed six exceptions to the rule (i.e., trills that should start with the main note):

1) When the trill starts *ex abrupto*
2) Qfter a staccato note or after a rest
3) On a repeated note when the repetition is thematic
4) When the melody skips and the trill is part of a characteristic interval
5) When melodic or harmonic outlines would be blurred, in particular where the movement of the bass would be weakened by the starting auxiliary
6) A fairly vague directive: Whenever an appoggiatura from above would be out of place[70]

In *Die Klavierwerke Bachs*, Hermann Keller agrees with Dannreuther's main note starts for freely entering trills and for characteristic intervals. He also adds two exceptions of his own: trills on organ-points in the bass and cases where the trill is preceded by its upper neighbor.[71] For Erwin Bodky, the only exception to the rule is where unpleasant parallels would result from an upper note start.[72] Walter Emery simply applies the rule to the "vast majority of Bach's plain shakes."[73]

Many of the above exceptions have been challenged by various musicologists since they were proposed. For example, Donington refutes the exception of trills preceded by the upper neighbor with quotations from both C.P.E. Bach and Marpurg. The latter wrote, in 1765, that "if the upper note with which a trill should begin immediately precedes the note to be trilled, it has either to be renewed by an ordinary attack, or has, before one starts trilling, to be connected, without a new attack, by means of a tie to the previous note."[74]

Again holding a position of dissent, Neumann is determined to contradict the modern convention of upper note/on-the-beat trills. In "Misconceptions About the French Trill," he convincingly presents extensive documentation which indicates that in the Baroque period, while the upper note start was a preference, the main note start was at least a valid option in some cases. For example, Neumann shows that in 1668, Bacilly wrote about the upper note rule and then condemned it for its rigidity, stating that "good taste [goût] alone has to be the judge."[75] Furthermore, Jean Rousseau described four kinds of trills; two starting on the upper note and two starting on the principal note.[76] Similarly, Dandrieu (1729), Berard (1755), Duval (1764), and Lacassagne (1766), all describe various ways of executing trills which include those that start on the principal note.[77]

The on-the-beat portion of the rule is derived primarily from ornamentation tables. However, Neumann argues that ornamentation contains a strong element of irregularity involving subtle rhythmical nuances that simply cannot be expressed accurately through musical notation (e.g., ornamentation tables). He supports this with a 1736 quote from Montéclair:

> It is impossible to teach in writing how these ornaments should be performed, since the personal instruction of an experienced master is barely sufficient to do so, however... I shall try to explain them the least poorly that I am able to.[78]

---

70 Edward Dannreuther, *Musical Ornamentation* (London: 1893-1895) I: 165-166. Taken from Neumann, *Ornamentation* 313.

71 Hermann Keller, *Die Klavierwerke Bachs* (Leipzig: 1950) 34. Taken from Neumann, *Ornamentation* 313.

72 Erwin Bodky, *The Interpretation of Bach's Keyboard Works* (Cambridge, MA: Harvard University Press, 1960) 150.

73 Walter Emery, *Bach's Ornaments* (London: 1953) 38. Quoted in Neumann, *Ornamentation* 313.

74 F.W. Marpurg, *Anleitung*, (Berlin: 1765) I: ix, 7, 55. Quoted in Donington, *Interpretation* 245.

75 Bénigne de Bacilly, *Remarques curieuses sur l'art de bien chanter* (Paris: 1668) 178ff. Quoted in Neumann, "Misconceptions," *Essays* 184.

76 Jean Rousseau, *Méthode claire, certaine et facile pour apprendre à chanter* (Amsterdam: 1691) 54ff and *Traité de la Viole* (1687) 77ff. Taken from Neumann, "Misconceptions," *Essays* 185.

77 Neumann, "Misconceptions," *Essays* 185-186.

78 Michel Pignolet de Montéclair, *Principes de musique* (Paris: 1736) 78. Quoted in Neumann, "Misconceptions," *Essays* 187.

Neumann then goes on to present several examples from treatises by Rousseau, Loulié, Montéclair, Couperin, Foucquet, and Abbé le Fils that suggest the possibility of before-the-beat trills. The fact that these are all French sources is particularly striking in that it was the French who were primarily responsible for the gradual change in preference from the main note trill to the upper note trill in Germany during Bach's lifetime.

In another of Neumann's articles, "A New Look at Bach's Ornamentation," the author suggests four main categories of trills, the first of which has the conventional upper note/on-the-beat start:

1) The appoggiatura trill (whose emphasized auxiliary may or may not be extended in an *appui* [i.e., the first tone may be short or long]
2) The grace-note trill, starting with the unaccented auxiliary before the beat and stressing the principal note
3) The main note trill, which may or may not start with an *appui*
4) The partially or fully anticipated trill (starting on either the main note or the auxiliary)

To determine which is the best choice in a given situation, Neumann suggests leaving out the trill at first and deciding what other ornament would likely be used (listed in the left-hand column of the table below). The appropriate trill (listed in the right-hand column) is then applied to that situation.

| | |
|---|---|
| (a) long appoggiatura | appoggiatura trill with *appui* |
| (b) short appoggiatura | appoggiatura trill without *appui* |
| (c) grace note | grace-note trill |
| (d) none of these ornaments | main note trill, sometimes anticipated trill |

As was the case with dotted rhythms, my conclusion regarding the debate over trills is that every case must be taken individually. However, it does appear logical to consider the upper note/on-the-beat start (subsequently referred to as an appoggiatura trill) as a general rule and to treat all deviations as exceptions. I will now, therefore, discuss all cases in the unaccompanied violin works of Bach where an appoggiatura trill does *not* seem to be a logical choice of execution. I will also discuss several cadential trills which do not appear in the autograph manuscript but should be added nevertheless. Cadential trills are considered essential ornaments in Baroque music and, as Hotteterre said in 1707, "it is necessary to point out that trills or shakes are not always marked in musical pieces."[79] The addition of unmarked cadential trills is not a topic of controversy.[80]

## Sonata No. 1 in g minor

Adagio: On the downbeat of m. 4, the 8th-note G is a written out appoggiatura and is already the upper note/on-the-beat. Therefore, the trill on F♯ should start on the main note, either right on the second 8th-note beat or possibly before the second 8th-note beat as an anticipated trill. Similar cases, where main note trills are appropriate, appear in mm. 12 and 21. This interpretation is not congruent with Donington's beliefs. Citing the above quotation by Marpurg (page 76) as evidence, he claims that this type of ornament, known as the *tremblement lié* (where the trill is tied to its preceding upper neighbor) should be treated in accordance with the "rule" by holding over the upper neighbor as a suspension.[81] However, Neumann points out that this would only make sense (if at all) when the beat is marked by another voice.[82] For the trills in mm. 5 and 13, the preceding tied upper neighbors make main note starts the only logical choice.

Fuga; Allegro: Appoggiatura trills should probably be added to the cadential dotted figure on beat two of m. 24 as well as those on the fourth beat of both mm. 54 and 86.

---

79 Hotteterre 18. Quoted in Donington, *Interpretation* 241.
80 See, for example, Donington, *Interpretation* 241, where the author cites Bacilly, Tosi, Quantz, and Hotteterre, and Neumann, *Ornamentation* 338-339.
81 Donington, *Interpretation* 245.
82 Neumann, *Ornamentation* 333.

**Partita No. 1 in b minor**

Allemanda: The trills that occur in mm. 2, 5, 13, and 17 appear to be melodic in function rather than harmonic. In that upper note starts would disrupt the linear motion, main note trills seem to be more appropriate in these cases. *Tremblement lié* figures appear in mm. 7, 18/b. 4, and 23, suggesting the likelihood of main note trills or the possibility of anticipated trills. An appoggiatura trill should probably be added to the cadential dotted eighth-note in m. 11.

Sarabande: An appoggiatura trill should probably be added to the cadential dotted quarter-note in m. 31.

**Sonata No. 2 in a minor**

Grave: The trills in mm. 1 and 17 are both preceded by their upper neighbors under a slur and are melodic ornaments within the descending linear motion. Therefore, they should both be played as main note trills. *Tremblement lié* figures are written in mm. 2/b. 2, 3/b. 4, and 15, and one should probably be added on the C♯ in m. 16/b. 2. Again, these figures suggest the likelihood of main note trills or the possibility of anticipated trills. Appoggiatura trills should probably be added to the cadential dotted figures in mm. 6, 11/b. 4 and 21.

In m. 22, the chromatic linear motion necessitates a main note trill on the D♯. Furthermore, it is important to note that the two wavy lines on the F and D quarter-notes in this measure are *not* trill symbols. Wavy lines were only used to indicate trills in Bach's keyboard works. In this case, the intended indication is most likely that of vibrato—which can be executed with either the left hand *or the bow*. In his music dictionary of 1703, Sébastien de Brossard describes the string players' tremolo (a word sometimes used interchangeably with vibrato at that time) as a pulsation of the bow which allows the performer to reiterate the same pitch several times with one bow stroke "as if to imitate the tremblant of the organ."[83] A wavy line over a note was often used to indicate such pulsations.[84] This practice is confirmed by several other treatises, both before and after Brossard's, such as those by Ganassi (1543), Farina (1627), Simpson (1659), Walther (1732), and Mattheson (1739).[85]

Fuga: Appoggiatura trills should probably be added to the cadential dotted figures on beat two in mm. 17, 44, 136, and 279.

Allegro: An appoggiatura trill should probably be added to the cadential dotted figure in m. 18.

**Partita No. 2 in d minor**

Sarabanda: A *tremblement lié* figure occurs in m. 4, suggesting the likelihood of a main note trill or the possibility of an anticipated trill. In m. 17, the trill appears to be melodic in function rather than harmonic. In that an upper note start would disrupt the linear motion, a main note trill seems to be more appropriate in this case. Neumann discusses the trills in mm. 9, 13, and 25, concluding that upper note starts could not have been intended because they would require "Paganinian" contortions of the left hand (e.g., holding the G in m. 9 with the third finger and trilling on the C♯ with the fourth finger). He seems to have overlooked the possibility in that measure of simply establishing a G-D fifth with the third finger on the downbeat and then trilling on the C♯ with the third finger. Contrary to Neumann's argument, appoggiatura trills in these measures are indeed feasible. The only question that remains is one of desirability. In each case, careful consideration should be given as to whether or not one wishes to emphasize the tritone, the effect of which would be weakened by an appoggiatura trill.

Ciaccona: The only printed trill in this movement occurs in m. 73. Because it is melodic in function and an upper note start would disrupt the linear motion, a main note trill seems to be more appropriate in this case. Furthermore, the same type of trill should probably be added to the B♭ 16th-note in the following measure in order to maintain the sequential pattern. There are several other instances where trills should most likely be added as well. For example, a *tremblement lié* figure could be created in m. 16 by adding a trill (either main note

---

83 Quoted in Neumann, *Ornamentation* 514-515.

84 See, for example, *Cesti's Pomo d'oro* of 1666, an excerpt of which is presented in Neumann, *Ornamentation* 515.

85 Neumann, *Ornamentation* 515-518.

or anticipated) to the C♯. Also, appoggiatura trills should probably be added to the cadential dotted figures in mm. 132, 184, 208, and 256. In reference to the last one (m. 256), Neumann prefers either a main note or a grace-note trill. He argues that because an F-E resolution is sounded at the start of the measure, an appoggiatura trill, with its F-E resolution would be redundant. However, because the bass note changes from G to A on the second beat, I feel that another F-E resolution does not sound redundant and that an appoggiatura trill is appropriate.

**Sonata No. 3 in C Major**

Adagio: The only printed trill in this movement occurs in m. 44. This is the only *tremblement lié* figure within the six works in which the beat where the trill occurs is marked in another voice. Donington's interpretation of tying the appoggiatura over into the next beat now becomes a viable option—and my suggested execution. Another *tremblement lié* figure could be created in m. 14 by adding a trill (either main note or anticipated) to the A on beat 3. Finally, appoggiatura trills should probably be added to the cadential dotted figures in mm. 11 and 39.

Largo: The trills in mm. 6, 16, and 17/b. 1 are all melodic in function and are situated within stepwise descending lines. In that appoggiatura trills would disrupt the linear motion, main note trills seem to be more appropriate in these cases. Furthermore, the same type of trill should probably be added to the C 16th-note in measure 7/b. 1 in order to maintain the sequential pattern. *Tremblement lié* figures occur in mm. 9/b. 2 and 12, suggesting the likelihood of main note trills or the possibility of anticipated trills. The brevity of the B♭ on beat 3 of m. 2 indicates that a grace-note trill might be the best solution. For this execution a C-E-C triple-stop must be sounded before the beat. Similarly, a C-G double-stop before beat 3 in m. 8 is a viable solution. Although both an appoggiatura and a main note trill are technically feasible in m. 21, careful consideration should be given as to whether or not one wishes to emphasize the B♭-E tritone, the effect of which would be weakened if an appoggiatura trill were chosen.

**Partita No. 3 in E Major**

Preludio: An appoggiatura trill should probably be added to the cadential dotted figure in m. 135.

Loure: The trilled F♯ in m. 1 is part of a melodic sequence of descending thirds. A main note start would preserve the linear motion better than an appoggiatura trill, although the latter is not at all displeasing to the ear. Because of the melodic function and the brevity of the trilled note in m. 14, a main note start is advisable in this case. *Tremblement lié* figures occur in mm. 15 and 24, suggesting the likelihood of main note trills or the possibility of anticipated trills. The appoggiatura trill in m. 22 should probably have D-natural (as opposed to D♯, which is implied by the key signature) as the auxiliary pitch because it is an anticipation of the ensuing D-natural in the following measure.

Gavotte en Rondeaux: The major justification for the upper note/on-the-beat trill in Baroque music is that the upper note is a discord and the main note is the resolution of that discord. In the case of the trill in this rondo theme, however, the *main* note, G♯, forms a discord with the bass, A, and the upper note is actually a consonance (A-A octave). Therefore, the trills in mm. 1, 17, 41, 65, and 93 should probably begin with the principal note. The same reasoning applies to the trill on D♯ in m. 37. Appoggiatura trills, however, should probably be added to the cadential dotted figures in mm. 39 and 63.

**Summary:**

The *Three Sonatas and Three Partitas* of Johann Sebastian Bach are indisputably the pinnacle of the solo violin repertoire. Studying and performing them is a monumental task; a rite of passage for the serious violinist. With all the contradictions, disagreements, and ambiguities among musicians, both in Bach's time and in more recent times, it is impossible to conclude that there is only one way to perform these works. Knowledge of urtext editions, historical treatises, modern scholarly interpretations of those treatises, and internal evidence within the music must all be combined to interpret these complex and ingenious pieces successfully. As with any other piece of music, one of our primary concerns must be to present the sonatas and partitas the way the composer intended. Although it will never be possible to know exactly how Bach wanted these pieces to sound, it is hoped that this essay will help lead performers to interpretations that at least do the music justice. Perhaps the best we can hope for is that if Bach were around to hear one of our performances—he would enjoy it.

# APPENDIX A:

## Vibrato

String players today tend to apply a more or less continuous vibrato to almost everything they play. It is a topic of controversy as to whether this is appropriate for music of the 17th and 18th centuries. Some argue that vibrato should not be used at all in Baroque music; others feel that it should be used only occasionally as a type of ornament; and still others condone the use of continuous vibrato. This controversy has been going on for at least three hundred and fifty years. Marin Mersenne, in *Harmonie Universelle* (1636-7), wrote that "the tone of the violin is the most ravishing [when the players] sweeten it…by certain tremblings [vibrato] which delight the mind."[86] Later in the book he added:

> The verre cassé [vibrato] is not used so much now [on the lute] as it was in the past because the older ones used it almost all the time. But [it can not be dispensed with and] must be used in moderation…the left hand must swing with great violence.[87]

Over a century later, Leopold Mozart voiced a similar opinion. In his 1756 treatise, he describes the vibrato technique and recommends its use. He does, however, frown upon its *incessant* use, noting that there are performers "who tremble [vibrate] consistently on each note as if they had the palsy."[88] Sources such as these verify that during the Baroque period, some string players considered vibrato a type of ornament and used it in moderation, while others used it more or less continuously. The latter notion is further confirmed by statements such as the following one by Francesco Geminiani. In the 1751 text entitled the *Art of Playing on the Violin*, Geminiani explains the vibrato technique and says that when it is used, even on short notes, "it only contributes to make their sound more agreeable and for this reason it should be made use of as often as possible."[89]

We can thus assert that the argument that vibrato did not exist in the 17th and 18th centuries and that it should not be used at all in music of that time is completely unfounded. In fact, there are musical treatises describing vibrato that date back to 1529. The first known descriptions of vibrato for string instruments appear in Martin Agricola's *Musica Instrumentalis Deutsch* of 1529 and Sylvestro di Ganassi's *Regola Rubertina* of 1542.[90] Other early sources describing vibrato are those written by Mersenne (1636-7), John Playford (1654), Christopher Simpson (1659), Thomas Mace (1676), Marin Marais (1686), and Jean Rousseau (1687).[91]

Although it is certain that we should use vibrato when playing music of the Baroque period, the *extent* to which it should be used is—and always has been—simply a matter of personal taste. This being said, it is also important to consider the differences in sound between what may have been created on Baroque instruments and what is possible on those of today. We can deduce that Baroque violins were not equipped with either chin rests or shoulder rests in that neither paintings nor treatises of the time evidence their existence.[92] Therefore, the left hands of Baroque players must have been more involved with supporting the violin than those of modern players. For this reason, it is not likely that a player in the Baroque period, even one vibrating vigorously, could produce as fast or wide a vibrato as that which can be produced using modern equipment. The reader is encouraged to try vibrating on his or her violin without a chin rest or shoulder rest. The result may be close to what vibrato sounded like in Bach's time.

---

86 Marin Mersenne, *Harmonie Universelle* (Paris: 1636-7) trans. R.E. Chapman (The Hague: 1957) Book II, sect. on Lute ornaments 24. Quoted in Donington, *Interpretation* 232.

87 Mersenne 109. Quoted in Donington, *Interpretation* 232.

88 Mozart 203.

89 Francesco Geminiani, *The Art of Playing on the Violin: 1751*, ed. David D. Boyden (London and New York: Oxford University Press, n.d.) 8.

90 Robert Donington, *A Performer's Guide to Baroque Music* (New York: Charles Scribner's Sons, 1973) 85. The edition used for the Agricola was dated 1545, the original apparently being lost.

91 Donington, *Interpretation* 232-233.

92 The *New Harvard Dictionary of Music* places the development of the modern chin rest during the first quarter of the 19th century, perhaps by Louis Spohr, who illustrated it in his *Violinschule* of 1832. Randel 156-157.

## APPENDIX B:

### Fingerings

As discussed in APPENDIX A, we can deduce that Baroque violins were not equipped with either chin rests or shoulder rests in that neither paintings nor treatises of the time evidence their existence.[93] Therefore, the left hands of Baroque players must have been more involved with supporting the violin than those of modern players. We can further deduce that shifting from position to position, especially downward, must have been significantly more difficult without the aid of a chin rest or shoulder rest. For this reason, I believe that Baroque players probably kept shifting to a minimum and would probably not choose to play a passage in higher positions on lower strings that could more easily be played in lower positions on higher strings. This should be kept in mind when choosing a fingering for any given passage. The reader is encouraged to try shifting on his or her violin without a chin rest or shoulder rest.

## APPENDIX C:

### Bowing Styles

Within the thirty-two movements that make up Bach's unaccompanied violin works, there is not a single dot of articulation indicated. This does not mean that every note should be played legato. Although the slower pieces should be executed rather broadly, the faster movements should be played in a somewhat detached, clear, and crisp manner. In his essay of 1753, C.P.E. Bach writes:

> In general the briskness of allegros is expressed by detached notes and the tenderness of adagios by broad, slurred notes…even when a composition is not so marked.[94]

Quantz's essay of 1752 supports this view. There it is written:

> In the Allegro the quick passage-work must be played above all roundly, correctly, and distinctly, and with liveliness and articulation [meaning somewhat detached].[95]

The particular bow stroke that one should use to achieve the desired articulation is perhaps one of the most controversial issues among string players today. Some use the spiccato in the lower part of the bow, while others prefer the martelé stroke near the tip. (In fact, some use spiccato in the lower part of the bow and *call* it martelé.) Regardless of the terminology used, the best place to play articulated eighth-notes in a Baroque allegro is probably somewhere in the middle of the bow. In his 1760 letter to Maddalena Lombardini, Tartini recommends practicing rapid notes in the upper part of the bow and in the middle, but makes no mention of using the lower part of the bow.[96] In addition, Francesco Geminiani, in his *Art of Playing on the Violin* (1751), suggests that rapid eighth-notes are to be played "plain," and that "the bow is not to be taken off the strings." He does mention, however, "a staccato, where the bow is taken off the strings at every note,"[97] but this should probably be used at moderate speeds and for special effect only. David Boyden, the author of *The History of Violin Playing: From Its Origins to 1761* (1965), concludes that the bow stroke of the early 18th century produced a lighter and more clearly articulated tone than that of the present day. He writes:

> A kind of non-legato stroke must have resulted from the rapid wrist articulation of fast notes, approaching the modern *spiccato* in effect, but attained without actually leaving the string. There is no evidence of the modern *serré* stroke or the *martelé*, and these strokes

---

93 See preceding footnote.

94 C.P.E. Bach 149.

95 Quantz 129.

96 Giuseppe Tartini, *A Letter from the Late Signor Tartini to Signora Maddalena Lombardini (Now Signora Sirmen)*, trans. Dr. Bumey (New York and London: Johnson Reprint Corporation, 1967) 17.

97 Geminiani 8.

are out of place in Baroque music, much as chromium would be in the furnishings of an eighteenth-century coach-and-six.[98]

The following passage from Donington's *The Interpretation of Early Music* seems to present a viable approach to performing a Baroque allegro with modern instruments.

> Where no special effect is intended, and the passage is rapid, but of average intensity, a very relaxed and easy style is required. The bow should be allowed to ease off its pressure on the string between each note by its own natural resilience, without actually being allowed to spring clear of the string. This is half-way between the violinist's detache (which is in fact a legato but with separate bows) and his spiccato (with the bow springing clear of the string and back again): a convenient term for this is sprung detache; and it will be found quite invaluable in countless ordinary baroque allegros. It can be combined with the [slightest pressure of the forefinger on the stick of the bow], or not, according to the degree of incisiveness desired.
>
> At slower speeds, a slightly sprung detache will still be found useful, but beyond a certain slowness it is not suitable. The crisp finger-pressure can then be used alone, if sharpness is still desired; but the slower the passage, the greater the probability that its general character will be cantabile and legato.
>
> The best part of the bow at which to take an average succession of moderate or rapid notes is about one-third from the point of the bow. Nearer the point, they are apt to sound a little insubstantial; nearer the heel [frog] they are apt to sound too ponderous...There is no doubt at all that the modern usage of taking them at the heel, in the hammered style with the bow lifted off the string between each note and returned to it with percussive force, is completely anachronistic and out of style. It produces an agitated impression far less brilliant and powerful, in spite of the energy displayed, than the relaxed but vital flow of notes intended by the baroque teachers.[99]

## APPENDIX D:

### Ritardandos

The issue of ritardandos in Baroque music seems to be one of some contention. Because ritardandos are generally not marked in Baroque music, some musicologists consider it taboo to place a ritard before final cadences.[100] However, there is sufficient evidence contained in contemporary treatises to support the legality of freedom of tempo and specifically the application of ritardandos before major cadences in Baroque music.

In 1614, Girolamo Frescobaldi wrote:

> The cadences, although they may be written quickly, are properly to be very much drawn out; and in approaching the end of passages or cadences, one proceeds by drawing out the time more adagio.[101]

---

98 David D. Boyden, *The History of Violin Playing: From Its Origins to 1761 and Its Relationship to the Violin and Violin Music* (London: Oxford University Press, 1965) 399.
99 Donington, *Interpretation* 538-539.
100 Neumann, "Baroque Treatises," *Essays* 5.
101 Girolamo Frescobaldi, *Toccate* (Rome: 1615-6) Preface 5. Quoted in Donington, *Interpretation* 433.

C.P.E. Bach wrote:

> In slow or moderate tempos, caesurae are usually extended beyond their normal length…This applies to *fermate*, cadences, etc., as well as caesurae. It is customary to drag a bit and depart somewhat from a strict observance of the bar…[102]

Some might see the following contradictory passage from C.P.E. Bach as proof that one should not apply ritardandos to final cadences.

> In affettuoso playing, the performer must avoid frequent and excessive retards, which tend to make the tempo drag. The affect itself readily leads to this fault. Hence every effort must be made despite the beauty of detail to keep the tempo at the end of a piece exactly the same as at the beginning, an extremely difficult assignment. There are many excellent musicians, but only a few whom it can be said truthfully that in the narrowest sense they end a piece as they began it. Passages in a piece in the major mode which are repeated in the minor may be broadened somewhat on their repetition in order to heighten the affect. On entering a *fermata* expressive of languidness, tenderness, or sadness, it is customary to broaden slightly.[103]

When seen in another light, however, this passage only confirms the use of cadential ritardandos. First, he warns against "frequent and excessive retards," which implies that occasional slight retards are acceptable. Furthermore, according to C.P.E.'s own account, there were more excellent musicians of the time that slowed down at the end of a piece than those that remained in strict tempo, whether he condoned it or not.

Although the word ritardando rarely appears at the end of a Baroque movement, it is not uncommon to see Grave or Adagio in the last few measures. Donington suggests that these terms, rather than indicating sudden tempo changes, were sometimes used to imply molto ritardandos (i.e., more of a gradual slowing down than one might do naturally). He cites an example for organ of J.S. Bach, the Fugue XV in c minor, in which the last section is already in an Adagio tempo, yet the word Adagio appears over the last half-measure. This example makes for a convincing argument that, at least sometimes, the word Adagio (or Grave) at the end of a movement may have been used to indicate a gradual slowing down, rather than a sudden tempo change. In any event, it is clear from contemporary treatises that occasional ritardandos applied at major cadences, even when not marked, are at least acceptable, if not obligatory.

## APPENDIX E:

### Quantz/C.P.E. Bach; German Text

**Quantz:**

Bei den Achtteilen, Sechzehntheilen, und Zwei und dreißigtheilen, mit Puncten, s. (c) (d) (e), geht man, wegen der Lebhaftigkeit, so diese Noten ausdrücken müssen, von der allgemeinen Regel ab. Es ist hierbei insonderheit zu merken: daß die Note nach dem Puncte, bei (c) und (d) eben so kurz gespielet werden muß, als die bei (e); es sei im langsamen oder geschwinden Zeitmaaße. Hieraus folget, daß diese Noten mit Puncten bei (c) fast die Zeit von einem ganzen Viertheile; und die bei (d) die Zeit von einem Achttheile bekommen: weil man die Zeit der kurzen Note nach dem Puncte eigentlich nicht recht genau bestimmen kann.

Diese Regel ist ebenfalls zu beobachten, wenn in der einen Stimme Triolen sind, gegen welche die andere Stimme punktirte Noten hat, s. (i). Man muß demnach die kurze Note nach dem Puncte nicht mit der dritten Note von der Triole, sondern erst nach derselben anschlagen. Widrigenfalls würde solches dem Sechsachttheil oder Zwölfachttheiltacte ähnlich klingen.

---

[102] C.P.E. Bach 375.

[103] C.P.E. Bach 161.

In dieser Tactart sowohl, als im Dreiviertheiltacte, bei der Boure, Sarabande, Courante, und Chaconne, müssen die Achttheile, so auf punctirte Viertheile folgen, nicht nach ihrer eigentlichen Geltung, sondern sehr kurz und scharf gespielet werden. Die Note mit dem Puncte wird mit Nachdruck markiret, und unter dem Puncte der Bogen abgesezet. Eben so verfährt man mit allen punctirten Noten, wenn es anders die Zeit leidet: und soferne nach einem Puncte oder einer Pause drei oder mehr dreigeschwänzte Noten folgen; so werden solche, besonders in langsamen Stücken, nicht allemal nach ihrer Geltung, sondern am äußersten Ende der ihnen bestimmten Zeit, und in der größten Geschwindigkeit gespielet; wie solches in Ouvertüren, Entreen, und Furien öfters vorkömmt. Es muß aber jede von diesen geschwinden Noten ihren besondern Bogenstrich bekommen: und findet das Schleifen wenig statt.[104]

## C. P. E. Bach:

Die kurzen Noten nach vorgegangenen Puncten werden allezeit kürzer abgefertiget als ihre Schreib-Art erfordert, folglich ist es ein Ueberfluß diese kurze Noten mit Puncten oder Strichen zu bezeichnen.

Seit dem häufigen Gebrauche der Triolen bei dem so genannten schlechten oder Vier Viertheil-Tacte, ingleichen bei dem Zwei- oder Dreiviertheil-Tacte findet man viele Stücke, die statt dieser Tact-Arten oft bequemer mit dem Zwölf, Neun oder Sechs Achttheil-Tacte vorgezeichnet würden. Man theilt alsdann die bei Fig. XII.

In der Schreibart der punctirten Noten überhaupt fehlet es noch sehr oft an der gehörigen Genauigkeit. Man hat daher wegen des Vortrags dieser Art von Noten eine gewisse Hauptregel festseßen wollen, welche aber viele Ausnahme leidet. Die nach dem Punct folgenden Noten sollen nach dieser Regel auf das kürzeste abgefertiget werden, und mehrentheils ist diese Vorschrift wahr: allein bald machet die Eintheilung gewisser Noten in verschiedenen Stimmen, vermöge welcher sie in einem Augenblicke zusammen eintreten müssen, eine Aenderung; bald ist ein flattirender Affect, welcher das diesen punctirten Noten sonst eigene Trokige nicht verträget, die Ursache, daß man bei dem Puncte etwas weniger anhält. Wenn man also nur *eine* Art vom Vortrage dieser Noten zum Grundsaße leget, so verliert man die übrigen Arten.[105]

---

[104] Johann Joachim Quantz, *Versuch einer Anweisung die Flöte traversiere zu spielen* (Kassel: Bärenreiter, 1974) 58-59 and 270. Johann Joachim Quantz, *On Playing the Flute*, trans. Edward R. Reilly (New York: Schirmer Books, 1985) 67-68 and 290-291.

[105] Carl Philipp Emanuel Bach, *Versuch über die wahre Art das Clavier zu spielen* (Leipzig: C.F. Kahnt, 1906) I: 89-90 and II: 65. Carl Philipp Emanuel Bach, *Essay on the True Art of Playing Keyboard Instruments*, trans. and ed. William J. Mitchell (New York: W. W. Norton, 1949) 157,160, and 372.

# BIBLIOGRAPHY

Aldrich, Putnam. "On the Interpretation of Bach's Trills." *The Musical Quarterly* 49 (1963): 289-310.

_____. *Ornamentation in J.S. Bach's Organ Works*. New York: Coleman-Ross, 1950.

Bach, Carl Philipp Emanuel. *Essay on the True Art of Playing Keyboard Instruments*, trans. and ed. William J. Mitchell. New York: W. W. Norton, 1949.

_____. *Versuch über die wahre Art das Clavier zu spielen*. Leipzig: C.F. Kahnt, 1906.

Bach, Johann Sebastian. *Six Sonatas and Partitas for Violin Solo*, ed. Ivan Galamian. New York: International Music Co., 1971.

_____. Sonatas and Partitas: BWV 1001-1006. Sigiswald Kuijken, Violin. Editio Classica, 77043-2-RG, 1990.

_____. *Three Sonatas and Three Partitas for Solo Violin: BWV 1001-1006*. ed. Günter Hausswald. Kassel: Bärenreiter, 1959.

Badura-Skoda, Paul. *Interpreting Bach at the Keyboard*, trans. Alfred Clayton. Oxford: Clarendon Press, 1993.

Baillot, Pierre Marie. *The Art of the Violin [1835]*, ed. and trans. Louise Goldberg. Evanston: Northwestern University Press, 1991.

Bodky, Erwin. *The Interpretation of Bach's Keyboard Works*. Cambridge, MA: Harvard University Press, 1960.

Boyden, David D. *The History of Violin Playing: From Its Origins to 1761 and Its Relationship to the Violin and Violin Music*. London: Oxford University Press, 1965.

Brown, Howard Mayer and Stanley Sadie. *Performance Practice: Music After 1600*. New York and London: W.W. Norton, 1989.

Butt, John. *Bach Interpretation: Articulation Marks in Primary Sources of J.S. Bach*. Cambridge and New York: Cambridge University Press, 1990.

Collins, Michael. "A Reconsideration of French Over-Dotting." *Music and Letters* (1969): 111-123.

Cyr, Mary. *Performing Baroque Music*. Portland, OR: Amadeus Press, 1992.

Dart, Thurston. *The Interpretation of Music*. London: Hutchinson, 1962.

Dolmetsch, Arnold. *The Interpretation of Music of the XVIIth and XVIIIth Centuries*. London: Novello, n.d. [1915].

Donington, Robert. *A Performer's Guide to Baroque Music*. New York: Charles Scribner's Sons, 1973.

_____. *String Playing in Baroque Music*. New York: Charles Scribner's Sons, 1977.

_____. *The Interpretation of Early Music*. New York: St. Martin's Press, 1963.

_____. *The Interpretation of Early Music*. New rev. ed. New York and London: W.W. Norton, 1989.

Fuller, David. "Dotting, the 'French Style' and Frederick Neumann's Counter-Reformation." *Early Music* 5 (1977): 517-543.

Geminiani, Francesco. *The Art of Playing on the Violin: 1751*. ed. David D. Boyden. London and New York: Oxford University Press, n.d..

Hefling, Stephen E. *Rhythmic Alteration in Seventeenth- and Eighteenth- Century Music:* Notes Inégales *and Overdotting*. New York: Schirmer Books, 1993.

Little, Meredith and Natalie Jenne. *Dance and the Music of J.S. Bach*. Bloomington and Indianapolis: Indiana University Press, 1991.

Mozart, Leopold. *A Treatise on the Fundamental Principles of Violin Playing [1756]*, trans. Editha Knocker. London and New York: Oxford University Press, 1948.

Neumann, Frederick. *Essays in Performance Practice*. Ann Arbor: UMI Research Press, 1982.

_____. "Facts and Fiction about Overdotting." *The Musical Quarterly* 63 (1977): 155-185.

_____. "Misconceptions About the French Trill in the 17th and 18th Centuries." *The Musical Quarterly* 50 (1964): 188-206.

_____. *New Essays on Performance Practice*. Ann Arbor: UMI Research Press, 1989.

_____. "Once More: The 'French Overture Style.'" *Early Music* 7 (1979): 39-45.

_____. *Ornamentation in Baroque and Post-Baroque Music: With Special Emphasis on J.S. Bach*. Princeton: Princeton University Press, 1978.

_____. "Rhythm in the Two Versions of Bach's French Overture, BWV 831," *Studies in Renaissance and Baroque Music in Honor of Arthur Mendel*. Kassel, 1974: 183-194.

_____. "The Dotted Note and the So-Called French Style." *Early Music* 5 (1977): 310-324.

_____. "The Overdotting Syndrome: Anatomy of a Delusion." *The Musical Quarterly* 67 (1981): 305-347.

_____. "The Use of Baroque Treatises on Musical Performance." *Music and Letters* 48 (1967): 315-324.

O'Donnell, John. "The French Style and the Overtures of Bach." *Early Music* 7 (1979): 190-196 and 336-345.

Pont, Graham. "French Overtures at the Keyboard: How Handel Rendered the Playing of Them." *Musicology* 6 (1980): 29.

Quantz, Johann Joachim. *On Playing the Flute*, trans. Edward R. Reilly. New York: Schirmer Books, 1985.

_____. *Versuch einer Anweisung die Flöte traversiere zu spielen*. Kassel: Bärenreiter, 1974.

Randel, Don, ed.. *The New Harvard Dictionary of Music*. Cambridge, MA and London: Harvard University Press, 1986.

Rangel-Ribeiro, Victor. *Baroque Music: A Practical Guide for the Performer*. New York: Schirmer Books, 1981.

Rousseau, Jean Jacques. *A Complete Dictionary of Music [1768]*. London: J. Murray, 1975.

Stowell, Robin. *The Cambridge Companion to the Violin*. London and New York: Cambridge University Press, 1992.

_____. *Violin Technique and Performance Practice in the Late Eighteenth and Early Nineteenth Centuries*. London and New York: Cambridge University Press, 1985.

Tartini, Giuseppe. *A Letter from the Late Signor Tartini to Signora Maddalena Lombardini (Now Signora Sirmen)*, trans. Dr. Burney. New York and London: Johnson Reprint Corporation, 1967.

_____. *Treatise on Ornaments in Music*, trans. Cuthbert Girdlestone. Celle and New York: Hermann Moeck, 1961.

Tureck, Rosalyn. *An Introduction to the Performance of Bach*. London: Oxford University Press, 1960.

Wolff, Christoph. *Bach: Essays on His Life and Music*. Cambridge, MA: Harvard University Press, 1991.

_____. Liner notes. J.S. Bach, Sonatas and Partitas: BWV 1001-1006. Sigiswald Kuijken, Violin. Editio Classica, 77043-2-RG, 1990.